ONE LAST FLING

by Robert Rahula

ALSO BY ROBERT RAHULA

NOVELS:
Messieurs
Panamaniac
Island of Misfits
Day Another Paradise In
Bathhouse Stories
Conversation in a Belgian Bar
All the Yage in Reno
Exigent Circumstances
Uninvited Guest
A Modest Summation of Things

POETRY:
Trigger Points
Dentro Del Corazón Bloqueada
Camino
Migration
I Sing the Body Politic
Wonderland
From Whose Bourn
Poemas Españoles
Expat Poems

ANTHOLOGIES:
Half Life
The Essential Dan Landes
Horror Stories for Children

One Last Fling

www.robertrahula.com

This is a work of fiction. Characters, organizations, businesses, products, locales, and events portrayed in this book either are products of the author's imagination or are used fictitiously.

First Printing, 2019

ISBN 978-1-7329708-4-7

Alma-gator Press

Barcelona • Madrid • La Chorrera

*"Thou hast committed fornication;
but that was in another country,
and besides, the wench is dead."*

-The Jew of Malta

Prologue

Ricardo was looking down the double barrel of seventy years of age. It was just a matter of time now. It had been—what?—seven years since he moved to Panama? He couldn't remember; he had lost track of time. He still returned to the States once or twice a year (mostly at his publisher's insistence) to handle various financial and legal matters, and to visit the few remaining friends he had. On this last trip back, he spent two days in New York City, meeting first with his publisher to review book sales, and then with his tax accountant to review (and pay) taxes. His publisher wanted to schedule a series of book signings to promote a recently-released anthology of Ricardo's short stories, but Ricardo said no. Book signings, which had once been so exciting when he was first getting published, now just left him feeling exhausted and weary. Plus, they no longer seemed necessary to him—his books seemed to be selling well enough. His accountant Harold Glass once again broached the idea of probate planning, but Ricardo just laughed it off and said that his probate plan was to die broke.

The day after those meetings, Ricardo traveled to Hamburg, New York, to visit his friend Carolina. While there, he walked the still-familiar streets of the city where he had written his first novel fifteen years ago. Seeing Carolina again was good, of course. But she, like everyone else he knew in the States, had moved on with her life. She was teaching full-time in a university now, and only had time to have dinner with him. Still, it was good to sit in one of their old favorite restaurants and talk and laugh together. But when they parted ways that night with a kiss, he wondered if he would ever see her again.

From New York, he flew to California and spent two nights there, in order to visit his old friend Marta. From there he flew back to Panama City. The cross-country detour to California from New York was grueling, and meant that his flight back to Panama would be longer, but he hadn't seen Marta in two years, and she had been his best—and sometimes only—friend and confidant for nearly thirty years.

Chapter 1:   The Old Man and the Semen

"What are your plans this year?" Marta asked him over lunch during his visit. They were sitting outside at a small table at a restaurant in Half Moon Bay, California. Ricardo could smell the salt air in the breeze. The sun was so bright that they both had to keep their sunglasses on. Ricardo also wore his old wide-brimmed hat, the same one he used in Panama, to protect his face. He had had some suspicious patches of sun-damaged skin removed from the side of his face a few years back. Luckily, they were benign, but ever since then, he never took chances with the sun.

"Well, I don't know," he said. "More of the same, I guess. I've started working on a new book. The working title is *The Old Man and the Semen*, but my publisher doesn't like that title."

Marta laughed and said, "I can't imagine why not. But what I meant was, what are your personal plans this year, aside from writing?"

"My personal plans? Hmmm." said Ricardo. He thought for a moment, then said, "Well, you know, a few years ago, I used to joke that the dating pool in which I swam consisted of two kinds of women: those who were looking for one last fling because their husbands had died, or those who were looking for one last fling because their husbands were still alive. But now, I find myself at the deep end of the same pool and there's no one left. So now I guess I'm the one looking for one last fling.”

“Are there only women in this pool?” asked Marta.

Ricardo laughed. “Well, no, of course not. I’m open for business as usual. All I’m saying is that the pickings are getting pretty slim.”

“What about Carolina? You wrote your last book about her.”

“Yeah, but I wrote a book about Alison, and one about Haley, and one about Eve, and a couple of others. That doesn’t mean they’re in the cards anymore. They’ve all moved on. Or, I’ve moved on. In any case, they’re no longer available. No, the next fling, if there is one, has to be with someone I haven’t even met yet.”

“What about that Marco fellow, the one who works in the restaurant down there?” Marta asked. “You sent me an email about him. He sounded nice.”

“Well, yes, there’s Marco. He’s a possibility. In fact, I would be very interested in pursuing him, but at my age one has to be careful.”

“What do you mean?”

“Well, I think he’s mid to late twenties. And yes, he seems to like me, but still... there’s a huge age difference.”

“You once told me that age difference is less important in the gay world. In fact, wasn’t there a huge age difference with you and Cody?”

True on both counts,” said Ricardo. “But I still have to see if Marco is interested. My answer to your question, however, is that aside from Marco, my wish for this year would be to have one last fling.”

“It seems to me, Ricardo, that you have more flings than anyone I know.”

“No, I’m not talking about affairs,” Ricardo said. “I mean one last fling in terms of a relationship... falling head over heels, you know... being madly in love.”

Marta looked serious. “Oh that,” she said. “Love... well, that’s more difficult.”

“I *know*,” Ricardo said.

“And why do you say *last* fling? Why not just

another fling?" Marta asked.

Ricardo looked at her. "Well, let's be honest, Marta. No one lives forever. I'm lucky now. My health is good. But eventually that will change."

"Well, first of all," Marta replied, "the years have been good to you. You could pass for mid-fifties. So you could always have one last fling, and then another last fling, and then another. You could be like the Grateful Dead with the never-ending final tour."

Ricardo laughed, and said, "Ah... beautiful lies. But thank you, nonetheless. I should be so lucky. But one year at a time, my friend, one year at a time."

Marta changed the subject. "Did you get to spend much time with Carolina while you were in New York?"

"Just dinner. She's got her hands full with her new job teaching at the university. But it was good to see her."

"I always thought the two of you would have made a good couple," Marta said.

"Well... there's that sex thing, you know." Ricardo explained. "We're great friends, but I guess she was never interested in sex with me... and you know me: great sex is just so central to my definition of a relationship."

"Uh huh... well, you know that changes with time," Marta said. "I mean, Tom and I have been married for eleven years now, and the sex is still good, but the love and companionship... just the day-to-day compatibility... is really what holds us together."

"I've read that," Ricardo said, "but it's never worked that way for me. I've got to be swept away by sex. If the sex gets boring, the relationship is over."

"Hmm... and you and Carolina never...?"

"Nope... I mean, we made out one time when we both were drunk, but that was it. I guess I never set her heart on fire. But you're right. We would have made for a fun couple if that had happened."

"Who else did you see this trip?"

"Besides you, Carolina, my publisher and my

accountant, nobody. There's no one left."

"What about Cody? Did you stop and see him?"

Ricardo felt sad. "No... he died a few years ago."

"Oh, I'm sorry. I didn't know that."

"Well, he was pretty old and not in good shape," said Ricardo. "I think his mind was gone for the last couple of years."

"I'm so sorry."

Ricardo shrugged. "That's life. You blink, and it's over."

Marta shook her head, thought for a second, and then asked, "What's the new book about?"

"I'm not sure yet. I'm still playing around with it. It started off as this weird dream I had about an old man who has magical semen. But I don't know how it's going to come out, I mean, how the *story* will come out, not the semen. I know how semen comes out. I'm still playing with the plot, but you know me, I just write and rewrite until some story emerges."

"So it's not a parody of Hemingway?" Marta asked.

"No," Ricardo laughed. "But I do like whimsical titles."

"Well, I look forward to it, as always."

"Thank you, Marta. You're the best."

As they continued to chat throughout lunch, fragments of memories kept floating up in Ricardo's mind, images of how they had met in that locked rehab center almost thirty years ago: Marta's arms swollen red with infected track marks; Ricardo's brain operating on its last raw wires; his stomach bleeding from too much alcohol; how they found each other shivering and vomiting in the hallway one dark night; and how they had helped each other through the subsequent horrible days. They had formed a bond there that had never been broken, despite the ensuing years in which each of them, in their own way, found separate success in life: Marta with her career and marriage, and Ricardo with his writing and self-exile to Panama. Marta had successfully gotten off drugs after only a few brief relapses. Ricardo still drank, but he had learned to keep it under control. But Marta's move to California with her husband and Ricardo's move to Panama meant that their in-person visits had dwindled over the years. The same thought occurred to Ricardo regarding Marta that had occurred to him the other night with Carolina: he wondered if he would ever see her again.

Chapter 2:   Marco

The flight back to Panama wasn't as bad as usual, mostly because Ricardo was able to sleep some on the plane, which normally he could never do. In Panama, he caught a direct bus to La Chorrera. In La Chorrera, he caught a local bus to Villa Rosario, the town where he had lived for six of the past seven years. It was almost five in the afternoon by the time he got back to his apartment. He took a hot shower, climbed into bed and despite his sleeping on the plane, slept twelve more hours, waking up at dawn to the sound of roosters crowing in the neighborhood.

He had had that dream again, but as usual, he could only remember pieces of it. There was this old man with the magic semen. Somehow Ricardo could see inside the old man's body, and the semen was electric blue with little sparkles. He could see it brewing and pulsating in the old man's testicles. Ricardo realized in the dream that the old man must be a brujo—a Latino sorcerer. What Ricardo had not told Marta, because he worried she might find it gross, is that what made the semen magical was that anyone who drank it became young again. It was logical that this would entail giving the brujo a blowjob, but Ricardo had never seen that in any of the dreams. He did one time get a fragment of an image of someone drinking the semen from a glass cup. And Ricardo was not sure if the magic semen made the drinker simply younger than they were, restoring vitality and good looks, or whether it gave the person everlasting life, that is, whether the effects were temporary or permanent.

But as always, there were only fragments of images,

and Ricardo awoke trying to piece them together. Usually there were one or two new images, and that was the case when Ricardo awoke on this particular morning: First, he had realized that the old man was a brujo; and second, he had the impression that when someone drank the magic semen, the old man became younger too. Ricardo thought about this as he got up to brew coffee. That meant that the old man had to have someone drink the magic semen for him to remain young. Odd, Ricardo thought. Also, he thought it odd that there was nothing sexual about the dream. He never saw any sex. He just saw the electric blue semen pulsating inside the old brujo's scrotum. The dream was as clinical as a medical journal article.

Once the coffee was ready, Ricardo climbed back into bed, propped up pillows, made a few notes in a dream journal he kept by the bed, drank his coffee and thought about the day ahead. He decided he would text Marco and see if he wanted to have lunch. He needed to check his bills online and pay any that were due. He also needed to send both Carolina and Marta thank-you emails. That last thought made him think of Marta's question of who else he had visited on his trip. His answer had been simple: there really wasn't anyone else to visit. He wondered if this was how it was for everyone—that the longer you lasted, the longer you outlasted everyone else. If you didn't die of natural or unnatural causes, he thought, maybe sheer loneliness would kill you. Still, here in Panama he had two or three friends. There was Miguel, who owned the restaurant Los Cuñados in La Chorrera. There was Jenny, who ran the best brothel in La Chorrera. There was Ted, Jenny's gringo husband and Ricardo's former landlord. There was Dan, a former L.A. cop, who had retired here years ago. Finally, there was young Marco who lived in Villa Rosario but worked in Miguel's restaurant. And there were, of course, a multitude of Panamanians who worked in various stores in Villa Rosario who knew him as a customer and always greeted him when they passed on the street. But of the whole group, Ricardo felt that only Miguel and Dan qualified as personal friends. Ted and Jenny were business friends, and Marco was still too new of an acquaintance.

Ricardo thought about Marco for a moment, then got up, went over to his writing desk and opened his laptop. While it was powering up, he refilled his coffee, then came back to the desk and sent Marco a Facebook message saying he was back in town and asking him to lunch. Then Ricardo climbed back into bed to drink more of his coffee.

Even though Villa Rosario was still a tiny, sleepy, dirt-road Panamanian village, technology had begun to invisibly seep into the town. When Ricardo first moved here six years ago, the apartment building that Ted owned and operated was the only place in town that had internet. And that was because Ted only rented to gringos, and he had to have internet to attract them. Ted griped about the installation costs, but it had paid off. His building usually had a 100% occupancy rate. In fact, the availability of Wi-Fi in Ted's apartments had been the deciding factor in Ricardo's decision to move to Villa Rosario. He loved the town, but if there hadn't been Wi-Fi available, he would have stayed in La Chorrera. But soon, other buildings had started adding internet and eventually Ricardo moved to his present apartment, which was quiet, up on the second floor with a nice balcony view of the central valley outside the town.

Ricardo heard the ding of a reply message on his computer. He got up and checked the message—it was from Marco, saying yes to lunch, and asking where and when. He had written, "Me encantaría. ¿Dónde y cuando?" Ricardo texted him back, "11:30, en la Cantina del Mariscos," indicating a small seafood lunch place in town. A few seconds later, Marco texted back his agreement, and Ricardo climbed back into bed again.

He thought about Marco as he sat lay propped up in bed drinking his coffee. Marco's skin was a café con leche color with a few freckles on his cheeks. He had big dark eyes and full lips. He had an average build for a Panamanian, which is to say slimmer and shorter than Ricardo. His features and gestures were slightly effeminate, which Ricardo found attractive. In fact, Ricardo was very turned on by Marco. Over the past few months, therefore, he had gradually questioned Marco about his sexual history, medical history and safe sex practices. Ricardo felt it would be safe to have sex with Marco. But there was more than just physical attraction. It was Marco's friendly and intelligent conversation that Ricardo liked best. He felt at ease with Marco—more than at ease—he felt drawn in. He wanted to be closer to Marco, personally and emotionally, as well as physically. But, as he had told Marta over lunch just two days earlier, there was a big difference in their ages, spanning maybe as much as forty years. On the other hand, Ricardo thought, Marco might be ten years older than he looked. Ricardo had always found it hard to tell a Panamanian's age.

He had mentioned this to Marta the other day during their lunch at Half Moon Bay:

"Hell, Marta, he could be thirty-five, for all I know. I've never asked him his age, because I didn't want him asking me mine. I really want to take him to the Hotel de Sevilla in Playa Lenora, but I'm afraid to ask him because I think he'll turn me down because of the age thing."

Ricardo had told Marta about the Hotel de Sevilla before. It was a private clothing-optional gay hotel located near the remote beach of Lenora.

Marta laughed. "Are you telling me that the famous writer señor don Ricardo is afraid to ask someone out on a date because they might say *no*?"

Ricardo wagged a finger playfully. "First of all, I'm *not* famous. Marco doesn't even know about my books. Secondly, taking someone to that particular hotel is not exactly a *date*. It would be clear the minute we got there that it was basically a gay sex hotel. That would be like taking a girl to a brothel for a first date."

"Look, Ricardo, from everything you've told me, Marco is no innocent kid. He's a grown man, relatively sophisticated, who is perfectly capable of deciding who he likes and who he wants to sleep with. Just ask him. The worst that can happen is that he says no... or maybe the worst that can happen is that he says yes, but when you two get there, for whatever reason you don't have sex. But it's still a nice hotel on the beach. And from what you tell me, there's great eye-candy there. Bottom line Ricardo, I think you're being overly sensitive. Just ask him!"

Ricardo felt encouraged by Marta's advice. That night, while he was still in California, he emailed the hotel to see if there were any rooms available. An hour later, they emailed back indicating that they were currently full, but they had a room available the following Sunday, and it would be available for four nights. Ricardo emailed back with his credit card number saying he would take it for two nights. He did that to hedge his bet. If Marco declined his offer, he would still have two nice nights at the hotel. If Marco accepted his offer, but things didn't go well, he would only be stuck there for two nights. If things *did* go well, he might be able to extend the stay an extra day or two.

Ricardo finished his coffee and decided that he had stayed in bed long enough. He got up to shower. As he stepped out of the shower and dried off, he considered his body in the mirror. No, it was not a young man's body. Maybe, as Marta said, he could still pass for mid-fifties. But he wondered what Marco would think. Would Marco care? Would he be repulsed? And regardless of what Marco thought, would Ricardo be able to tell? So much of Panamanian culture was shaped by politeness, by never being direct, by always keeping things vague.

Ricardo wondered how he would broach the subject of the hotel with Marco. He decided to first show him some of his cell phone photos of the place, ones he had taken on his last visit. After he had dried himself and got dressed, he looked through his cell phone and picked out some photos, ones that showed the hotel building from the inside with its ornate Spanish design and its beautiful garden, plus ones that showed the pool that overlooked the beach, and a few pictures showing the rooms. He intentionally selected photos of the pool that showed the naked men in the pool, as well as pictures of the huge multi-colored gay flag waving in the garden.

After a small breakfast, Ricardo spent his morning, as usual, writing. This particular morning he was not working his *Old Man* book. Rather, he was working on a short story that he had started before he had left for his trip to the States. It was about an introverted woman named Cindy, whose boyfriend cajoles and manipulates her into having a threesome with a woman named Sarah, but then Cindy discovers she likes making love to a woman more than the sex she had been having with her boyfriend. She then arranges to meet secretly with Sarah again, and just the two of them make love. Ricardo already knew that the story would have to somehow end with Cindy leaving the boyfriend for Sarah, but he was having difficulty with the middle part, with Cindy's internal dialogue describing why she enjoyed a woman's body better than a man's. He worked on the story slowly, word by word for almost two hours. Then he took a break, stretched a bit, heated up his coffee in the microwave and then sat back down and re-read the last paragraph of what he had written:

Cindy couldn't believe she had orgasmed just by Sarah's hand between her legs, rubbing her clit with her forefinger and sliding her other fingers in and out of her vagina, all the while lying together kissing and sucking each other's tongues. Dave had never taken her to orgasm simply by touching her. As Cindy began to cum, Sarah pressed her lips hard against Cindy's mouth so that they shared the same breaths as Cindy began to involuntarily take short gasps of air, panting, almost hyperventilating. Sarah's other arm was around Cindy's neck, holding her head to Sarah's mouth. Cindy had one hand on Sarah's breast and the other in between Sarah's legs feeling the wet silky hair all around Sarah's vagina. As Cindy was about to cum, Sarah shoved her tongue as far into Cindy's mouth as she could. Cindy accepted it, surrendered to it, and tightened her lips around it to hold it in. She squeezed her eyes so tight that all light disappeared. And then the orgasm hit, and Cindy had to forcefully pull her head back to suck in oxygen, and then she let out a long moan and an "Oh God" and fell limp.

Ricardo was not happy with it. He wanted to shift the

focus back to the comparison that inevitably happens when one has a new lover. And he wanted to somehow convey the emotion of Cindy's sex rather than just the mechanics of it. He started typing:

> *She wasn't sure how long she lay there, limp as a ragdoll, but eventually she felt a cool breeze of air between her legs. Cindy lifted her head to see that Sarah had shifted down on the bed, holding her head about two inches from Cindy's crotch and blowing softly up and down on the lips around Cindy's vagina.*
>
> *Cindy let her head fall back and let out another "Oh God". Sex with Sarah was so different. Sarah's body was so smooth, not like Dave's hairy and coarse skin. Sarah's body was soft, yet firm, responsive, and warm. And breasts... Cindy had never fully appreciated why men were so fixated on women's breasts, but now, having played with Sarah's breasts, having kissed and sucked those nipples, having felt them pressed against her own body, now she understood how sexual they were. Dave always wanted her to suck on his nipples, and Cindy did it to oblige him, but it did nothing for her. They were just flat man-nipples, like buttons with a bump in the middle, not long and warm and responsive like Sarah's.*
>
> *And then there was the joy of not having to deal with Dave's penis, not having to do things to get him hard, not having to watch her timing, not having to avoid saying anything that he could misconstrue in any way as disappointment, not having to worry about being lubricated enough, not having to always let him be on top because that's what he liked, not having to deal with his yucky cum and his fascination with cumming on her breasts or in her mouth, or that one horrid time, on her face. She hated the taste of cum, the thick salty gunk that made her want to gag when he insisted on finishing in her mouth and wanted her to swallow it. And not having to deal with the risk of pregnancy when he wanted to fuck! Now she could stop taking those birth control pills which made her feel so bloated, just because Dave didn't like*

condoms.

God damn it! She realized that she hated Dave.

Sarah moved up to Cindy's face.

"Are you okay?" Sarah asked softly.

Cindy lifted one hand, wrapped it around Sarah's waist, that slim, soft, smooth waist, and pulled Sarah close to her, and kissed her on the mouth.

"Yes, my love," she said, "I'm very much okay."

Ricardo read through what he had written again and considered it again. It still needed a lot of work. It's odd, he thought. No matter how many women a man makes love to in his life, he never really knows how they feel, what they think, what they really experience. He thought back to the women he had had sex with. While they were all different in feel, touch, taste, and sexual preference, the single common element in each and every one of them was that they always remained a mystery to him. They came into his life, and they went out of his life. And when they disappeared, Ricardo was always left clawing at the air for clues as to who they really were. It was like trying to grasp will-o'-the-wisps, phantoms, or smoke. He looked up at the clock. It was close to the time he should leave if he wanted to meet Marco. He saved what he had written and closed his laptop. He would work on it more this afternoon. But in the meantime, he had some business to attend to.

When he got to the restaurant, Marco was waiting at one of the outside tables under the shade of an overhanging tin roof. They exchanged small talk for a while until the waitress appeared to take their orders. After she disappeared into the kitchen, Ricardo started to describe the Hotel de Sevilla.

"Do you know the Hotel de Sevilla?" Ricardo asked in Spanish. "That little gay hotel in Playa Lenora?"

"I have heard of it, of course," said Marco. "I understand it's very nice."

"I've been there. It *is* very nice."

"Really?" said Marco.

Ricardo pulled out his cell phone and showed Marco the photos he had previously selected.

"What a beautiful place," said Marco.

"It's *very* nice," Ricardo said again. "I know there are some gay hotels in Panama City that have nice pools, but this is the closest one to here that is on a beach. I'm going to take the bus there this next Sunday, just for two nights. There's one bus that leaves from here every day at noon. It only takes three hours to get there and there's a bus stop about three hundred meters from the hotel. Would you like to come with me?"

"Oh, amigo. It looks very expensive."

"No, no, Marco. I've already paid for the room. The cost to me is the same whether you come or not. You can stay with me for free. There is a restaurant in the hotel and some sandwich places on the beach. I'll pay for your meals. That would be my treat. But I would enjoy your company." Ricardo looked at Marco for some sort of sign, then decided to be a bit more transparent. "The place is usually full, so I was lucky to get the last room. And the rooms only have one large bed, but we can both fit, and I don't snore loudly, I'm told. So please, be my guest, Marco."

He could see Marco's eyes glance down left and right for a microsecond. Then Marco's face lit up with a broad smile. "Yes, don Ricardo. I would like that very much. Thank you!"

And that was how Ricardo got Marco to go with him to Hotel de Sevilla. Later that night, Ricardo wondered if he was turning into one of those old gay men who hang around foreign towns in hope of luring young gay men by taking advantage of their economic differences. He didn't want to be one of those guys. But he reassured himself that his relationship with Marco seemed to be based on friendship and mutual liking. It was true that he often paid for Marco's meals when they had lunches, but Marco would occasionally pay for his own meal when he had money. Marco's income varied depending on the tips he received working as a waiter in Miguel's restaurant. Once, on a day after he had waited on a large rowdy group of gringos, Marco was flush with cash, because they had tipped him well, and he was proud to be able to buy Ricardo's lunch.

But it was also true, Ricardo thought, that he had carefully planned how he was going to invite Marco to the hotel, and also true that the invitation was for the purpose of getting him alone in a room. But wasn't that always the nature of seduction? Had he not done the same with Alison years ago, and with Eve before that? Isn't that what dating always is—a careful dance of planned seduction? Love at first sight may be the theme of many songs, but in Ricardo's experience it was always love at first carefully-crafted and orchestrated seduction. Male or female, animal or bird, there's always the mating dance, the bringing of flowers or pretty stones... or in his case, a trip to the beach.

Chapter 3:   The Road to Sevilla

Getting to Hotel de Sevilla was not as easy as Ricardo had implied to Marco. It was true that one could get there by bus, and also true that there was a bus stop near the hotel. But what Ricardo chose not to mention was the fact that there was no direct bus route, nor were the roads paved. One had to change buses twice and the road was dusty and rocky with many switchbacks. Ricardo had always assumed that the location for Hotel de Sevilla was carefully selected to be out of the way, and difficult to get to. While Panama had a very tolerant official policy toward gays, it was still a very Catholic country, and discretion was always the better part of gay economic survival. The Hotel de Sevilla was known among gays as the nicest and most indulgent gay hotel in all of Panama, but that reputation was kept under cover, so to speak. There was no mainstream advertising, and the hotel always declined inclusion into regular tour books. There wasn't even a sign on the side of the hotel. Advertising was only on gay websites, and one had to access the hotel's website through those gay websites. This lack of mainstream advertising would doom any regular hotel, but the Hotel de Sevilla flourished despite—or perhaps, because of—its inaccessibility.

The hills that lay between Villa Rosario and the hotel could not be classified as mountains, but the only access to the hotel was through those rocky hills on that narrow dirt road, and the trip could be exhausting. During the ascents and descents through the hills, the bus driver never got out of first gear. The windows were all open in hopes of fresh air to relieve the heat, but that resulted in filling the bus with road dust. For tourists flying into Panama City, the hotel would send a comfortable, air-conditioned van. The ride was not cheap, but all the clientele paid it. It was the only comfortable way to get there. But for gays living in Panama, because of either location or price, there was only the local bus.

Despite its remoteness, the hotel was usually full. And it was not only gay men who were loyal customers. The hotel was extremely liberal. Lesbian couples were welcomed, as well as bisexual and polyamorous couples. On occasion, one would see such guests. However, there were clear warnings in the website descriptions that the hotel was clothing optional, and that while all were welcomed, anyone who might be offended by seeing naked men occasionally having sex anywhere on the hotel grounds might not find the culture of the hotel to their liking.

On Saturday, Ricardo texted Marco and described the bus route they would take in more accurate detail, so that Marco would be prepared. They met as planned by the Parque Central in Villa Rosario that Sunday at 11:30 and caught the noon bus out of town. Three hours and two buses later, they arrived at the bus stop three hundred meters from the Hotel de Sevilla. Ricardo had taken this trip many times before, and it was arduous, but this time he enjoyed it because it gave him and Marco time to talk. They talked as most traveling couples do, commenting on each little farm or scene that they passed, and exchanging bits of their own personal histories between comments on the scenery. Because of all the bumps and twists and turns of the bus, their arms and legs were constantly touching, and neither one pulled away from the touch. Other than that, you would not have known that they were anything but good friends taking a long bus ride together. Finally, by the third bus, they arrived at a certain place in the road that Ricardo knew well, and he reached up and pushed the *parada* button to notify the driver to let them off.

The road they were on was constructed on the side of the last hill that led down to the beach. To the unknowing eye, the bus stop by the hotel seemed to be a stop in the middle of nowhere. There was simply the dirt road, trees and jungle, a broken pole where a bus sign used to be attached, but no bus bench and no other indication of a bus stop. The only mark of human presence was a high wall beside the road, covered in old vines and hidden by shrubs and small trees. The wall was painted dark green to blend in with the vegetation. If you weren't looking carefully, you wouldn't even know there was a wall there.

Marco looked around with a bit of apprehension as they stepped off the bus. "Are you sure this is the right place, don Ricardo?"

"Trust me, Marco," Ricardo replied, and pointed the direction that they should walk.

A few minutes later they came to a place where the wall was cleared of vegetation, and there was a door with an intercom speaker. Ricardo pressed the buzzer, identified himself, and the door buzzed open to let them in.

Inside, a magnificent garden confronted them, with a curved Spanish archway leading to the reception desk. Marco looked around in amazement. The garden was constructed to take full advantage of the fact that the hotel was built into the cliff overlooking the ocean about two kilometers below. Colorful flowers lined the inside wall that curved around the garden. Palm trees shaded lounge chairs and benches throughout the grounds. But Marco's eyes were drawn to the large swimming pool at the end of the garden, whose far edge merged with where the cliff dropped off, causing the edge of the pool to disappear into the view of the ocean in the distance, becoming an infinity pool. In the pool, several naked men were paddling about or standing in the chest-deep water talking with each other. Around the pool were white lounge chairs with umbrellas where other men lay, some naked, and some in bathing suits. On the left side of the garden were the various rooms, all in white stucco, each with unique wooden doors.

Marco just stood there looking around. Ricardo chuckled and poked Marco's arm. "Come on, let's go check in."

Inside the office, Carlos, the day receptionist, greeted Ricardo. "Hola don Ricardo, welcome back."

"Thank you, Carlos, it's good to be here. This is my friend Marco."

"Hola, Marco. Good to meet you."

"Mucho gusto," Marco replied.

They sat down, and Ricardo and Marco each produced their identity cards, as required by law when checking into a hotel. Ricardo also gave Carlos his credit card. Each signed the registration forms, and Ricardo signed the credit card voucher. Carlos gave Ricardo the room key and asked in English, "Does your friend need the usual orientation?"

"No," Ricardo answered, "I'll take care of that."

Ricardo walked Marco to their room. The door faced the garden, and the balcony faced the ocean.

"Oh, don Ricardo, this is amazing!" said Marco.

Ricardo had to agree. The view *was* spectacular. In the distance the sun was low in the sky and light danced off the ocean water.

Once inside the room, Ricardo began to unpack his small knapsack. "Marco," he said, "let's take a shower. It was a long bus ride and I feel very dusty from it. We'll have time to hit the pool, and then we can get some dinner. How does that sound?"

"That sounds good, don Ricardo."

Ricardo had hoped that fate would allow them to shower together. He had fantasized about soaping up Marco's body, running his soapy fingers over Marco's cock and up around his ass. But when Ricardo looked at the shower, he saw it was a small one and would not hold both of them comfortably. Nonetheless, he recognized that this would be a test of some sort, in that this would be the first time they would be undressing in front of each other. Ricardo slipped off his shirt, pants, and underwear. Marco was still unpacking items from his knapsack. Ricardo headed into the bathroom and began to shower.

The hotel always had plenty of hot water, and it felt good to get clean after such a long, hot, and dingy bus ride.

He washed himself, then grabbed a towel and walked back into the room to dry off. Marco had taken off his shirt and pants but still had his underwear on. Ricardo dried himself in such a way that Marco could see his nakedness if Marco wanted to, but Marco simply asked if the shower was ready, and stepped inside the bathroom to shower.

"Oh well," Ricardo thought to himself. "We'll see how this goes." He finished drying himself and put his bathing suit on and sat down on the bed to wait for Marco.

After Marco had finished showering, he stepped back into the room, drying himself with a towel. Ricardo caught a quick glimpse of his cock. It seemed nice. Uncircumcised, but nice. Marco quickly slipped on his swimming trunks, and then said, "Ready."

Ricardo stood up, grabbed the keys, and walked towards the door. Marco followed him. But when Ricardo got to the door, he turned to Marco.

"Come here," he said, reaching out and putting his hand around Marco's waist and pulling him in close to kiss him on the lips. To Ricardo's surprise, Marco kissed him back, putting his tongue into Ricardo's mouth, kissing and sucking Ricardo's lips. They stood there for two or three minutes, not saying anything, just kissing hard. Finally, Ricardo pulled away.

"Wow," he said, "you're a good kisser!"

"You too, amigo," replied Marco.

Ricardo felt oddly torn between wanting to show Marco the pool at sunset and pushing him back towards the bed. He didn't want to simply rush in and take advantage of Marco, but damn, he did kiss well. He leaned in and kissed Marco again, but this time lighter. "Why don't we go to the pool and have a little swim? We'll be back here later."

"Okay, amigo," said Marco between kisses. "Whatever you want."

Ricardo's brain was out of sync with his body. Just as he was deciding to take Marco to the pool, he leaned in and kissed Marco again and then he reached down and felt Marco's cock. It was hard, sticking straight up, lying against his belly under his swimsuit. Ricardo ran his hand up and down it. It seemed like a very nice shape.

"Oh, you're hard," he said.

"That happens," Marco laughed.

But Ricardo's brain won out. He pulled away again, deciding to take things a bit slower. "Let's go have a little swim, cool off a bit."

Marco laughed again. "Okay, amigo."

When they got to the pool, there were still several men, in couples or groups, lying on lounge chairs talking with each other or sunbathing. Some were naked, but some had put their suits back on. One couple was in a hot tub next to the pool, but at this particular point, no one was in the water. Ricardo and Marco found two lounge chairs in the shade of a large palm in the corner of the pool area. The sun was still bright but leaning down towards the horizon. Already it felt a few degrees cooler than when they had arrived, although it would still be another hour until sunset.

"Would you like something to drink, Marco?" Ricardo asked.

"Yes, whatever you're having."

Ricardo went to the little bar off to the side of the pool and ordered two piña coladas. He showed them his room key, and the bartender had him sign for the drinks. Ricardo brought them back to Marco, and they lay there together in the shade watching the ocean and sipping at their icy drinks. Small clouds high above drifted by. It was a beautiful to gaze out for so many miles over the ocean, all the way to the horizon.

Ricardo placed his drink on the small plastic table next to his lounge chair. "I'm going into the water," he said to Marco. "Want to join me?"

"Oh no, I do not like cold water," Marco said.

"Oh no, Marco, this water is not cold. I promise you, it's just perfect."

"You go first, don Ricardo."

Ricardo knew from experience that the water would be perfect. He didn't know how they did it, but the water was always perfect. When the air was cold, the water was warm. When the air was hot, the water was just cool enough.

He walked down the steps into the water. And true to his experience, it was perfect. He paddled over to the corner near where Marco was sitting.

"See, Marco? It's perfect! Come on in."

Although it was clear when they first arrived that the men they had seen in the pool were naked, Ricardo chose to keep his swim trunks on. There was something about watching Marco getting ready to take his shower in the room earlier that told Ricardo that Marco was very shy. While he was responsive to Ricardo's advances, he was conservative in his nature. Ricardo had the intuition that it would be difficult for Marco to take his swimming trucks off in front of the other men—strangers—at the pool.

Marco put his drink down and walked into the water and paddled over to the side of the pool where Ricardo was standing.

"It *is* perfect!" he exclaimed.

"See, I told you," Ricardo said, slipping his arm around Marco's waist. Marco smiled and let himself be drawn in towards Ricardo, wrapping his arms around him. They kissed.

"Is okay to do this here?" Marco asked.

"Yes, believe me, no one cares. No one watches," Ricardo replied.

"Bueno," Marco said and pressed himself closer to Ricardo. They kissed more, and Ricardo could feel Marco's erection against his own. Ricardo thought to himself, *"This is going to be good."* He wanted to see that cock, take it in his mouth, suck it, run his tongue up and down its shaft, take it all the way down his throat. Who knew where this night would lead? He reached down to Marco's ass, grabbed it and pulled him even closer, kissing him hard. Marco kissed him back, thrusting his tongue in and out of Ricardo's mouth.

Ricardo was getting excited. It was unlike him to lose control, but he liked Marco and he liked what was happening. Still, he pulled himself away and swam over to the side of the pool that overlooked the ocean. Marco followed him and aligned himself next to Ricardo, facing the horizon, his front pressed against the pool wall, the water at chest height. Ricardo moved behind him, pressing his body against Marco, letting his own cock snuggle in between the cheeks of Marco's ass. He began to press his body into Marco's, and Marco pressed his pelvis back into Ricardo. Ricardo reached around and eased his hands down the front of Marco's bathing suit. There was that erect cock. And no hair. Evidently Marco shaved, and had shaved recently. The skin around his cock was smooth. His cock felt thick and hard. Ricardo put his mouth to Marco's ear.

"Okay, I can't stand this anymore. Let's go back to the room. We can take our drinks with us and come back here later and swim."

"Are you sure?" Marco replied.

"Yes. I want you in the room."

And so that's how it was. They left the pool, and walked hand-in-hand, back to the room, where they both stripped down, and Ricardo finally got to fully see Marco's cock, that thick, full, beautifully erect cock that seemed to follow the curve of Marco's body rather than stand straight out, and Ricardo finally got to take it into his mouth, down his throat, while Marco sucked him at the same time. It all felt so right, and Marco moaned when Ricardo took his balls into his mouth, and moaned more when Ricardo took his cock deep into his mouth again, and they both worked on each other in mad pleasure, touching each other everywhere, taking breaks to kiss when the sex got too intense, trying to hold off the orgasms as long as possible, but finally Marco's torso tensed up and he began to moan, and then he came and Ricardo got to swallow that glorious joy juice. Marco's body jerked and then he lay there for a moment, finally saying, "You are so good Ricardo. So good." He then he returned to Ricardo's cock and sucked it until Ricardo lost control, and started saying "oh fuck oh fuck oh fuck" in English, and then Ricardo came, and then they both collapsed back on the bed and just lay there, their hands touching each other's bodies and not moving.

"Coming" for Ricardo was never a sensation of arriving—to the contrary, it was the sensation of leaving, of disappearing, of losing control and all sense of bodily function, of being swept away into a large blue sea of nothingness, of surrender, total surrender to something so far beyond himself. The better the orgasm, the further he left his body. But the extent to which he could lose control always depended on how safe he felt with that particular lover. And somehow, even though it was their first time making love, Ricardo let himself go far out into the galaxy. And the further out he went, the longer it took him to come back and re-enter his body and regain control of his movements.

He and Marco must have lain there together just holding hands for almost thirty minutes. Finally, Ricardo was able to move again. He lifted his head and looked at the window. It was dark outside. He let his head fall back, turned to Marco.

"You okay?"

"Sí señor, estoy bien, y tú?" came the reply.

"I'm good, very good," Ricardo answered. He moved his arms and legs, and turned his head a few times. Then he said, with a note of surprise, "I'm hungry. Are you hungry?"

"Yes," Marco answered. "I am, a bit."

"Let's get up and get something to eat."

And so they did. They got up, got dressed and walked over to the hotel restaurant for dinner, holding hands and talking the way new lovers do. And Ricardo paid for that meal, and all the subsequent meals as he had promised. And later that night they fell asleep holding hands, and the next morning, after they had awakened and had coffee in their rooms, before they went over to have breakfast, Ricardo blew Marco again, loving that thick cock, and again swallowed that sweet cum, and later after going to the beach for the morning and eating lunch at one of the food shacks at the beach, and spending the afternoon at the pool, and returning to the room in the early evening, they made love before dinner again, and Marco took Ricardo's cock and sucked and stroked it until Ricardo came. The next morning their cocks were both a bit sore from so much sucking and coming that they agreed to simply kiss in bed before going to breakfast and then checking out and catching the bus for that exhausting ride back to Villa Rosario, except that this time they both fell asleep on the bus, because they were exhausted from so much sex, and so the bus ride was not so bad.

They got off the bus at Villa Rosario and shook hands goodbye by the Parque Central. Marco thanked Ricardo over and over for a great vacation, and Ricardo thanked Marco for accompanying him. And they promised to meet soon for lunch, and then they walked to their separate homes, Ricardo to his apartment, and Marco back to the home he shared with his mother and sister. And Ricardo realized later, he never did learn how old Marco was.

Chapter 4:   Carolina

Carolina's long email—two days later—came as a surprise to Ricardo. Since she had taken the job at the university last year, Ricardo had noticed that her emails had become shorter and less frequent, often containing apologies for not writing more, and explaining how busy the new world of academia was: a constant cycle of teaching, grading, advising students, working on committees, forming policy, not to mention university politics, and the petty backstabbing that seems endemic to all places of higher learning. When she had first taken the job, Carolina was amazed at how petty some of her fellow professors were. Ricardo had responded by quoting her that line about how the higher the monkey climbs, the more he shows his tail.

But this new email was long, almost two pages. It had arrived while Ricardo was sitting at his desk, outlining possible plot lines for his *Old Man* book. When he saw how long her email was, he saved what he had been writing, printed out her email, and took it outside to his balcony patio chair to read and ponder.

Evidently, Ricardo thought as he read the email, there was trouble, trouble right there in River City, as the old song goes. Carolina had been teaching a course in Gender Studies, and some students had complained that the course was not radical enough, while some other students had complained that the course was too radical. Idiots, Ricardo thought. But evidently the university had a policy of investigating any complaint no matter how spurious. So now Carolina's curriculum was "under investigation" by a committee comprised of four faculty members and two students. As a new professor, she was an at-will employee. Her contract could simply not be renewed at the end of the semester for any reason. So she was understandably nervous. She had spent almost five difficult years earning her PhD, and this was her first teaching job since graduating. Her email went into great detail about the course curriculum and the nature of the complaints. But Ricardo didn't really understand any of that. He was of the opinion that most of academia had lost its true purpose years ago and shifted to simply pandering to students and making money. He had once told Carolina jokingly that the only proper way to teach Gender Studies would be to throw all the students in a dark room naked for two hours a day, and then they could write a paper at the end of the semester about what they had learned.

It seemed to him that the complaints were stupid, and that Carolina was worried over nothing. So he skipped over the part in her email where she was explaining the philosophy behind her choice of curriculum and went to the important paragraph that followed. Spring break would be coming up this semester, and she would have two weeks off. She had been told that the investigation might take all semester, and she didn't want to stay in the city or around the University while the school was closed and the investigation was on hold—that it would just be a constant reminder of the sword of Damocles that was hanging over her head. So she was asking Ricardo in the email if she could come down to Panama and spend the two weeks with him.

Ricardo sat back and thought about this. Carolina had been a good friend for many years, starting when Ricardo had first moved to Hamburg, New York, to take a job as a probate lawyer. As he had explained to Marta at that lunch several weeks ago, he had been attracted to Carolina ever since he first met her, and at times had hinted to her about becoming more intimate. But there always seemed to be something—or someone—in the way. Either she had a boyfriend, or a girlfriend, or she was leaving to go somewhere, or starting a new job, or getting fired from an old job, or there was a crisis, or she was starting school. Eventually, Ricardo had decided that the continual sequence of obstacles and bad timing simply meant that she didn't want to fuck him. He reasoned that if people want to have sex, they usually find a way despite the worst obstacles. But he had accepted the situation, because he truly enjoyed her company and was very fond of her.

He didn't really understand why she was so stressed out, but if she wanted to come to Panama and visit him, why not? But then he thought about the dynamics of her coming to visit for two weeks. It's one thing to spend time with someone when each person has their own apartment, their own jobs, and other friends. But her coming to Panama would throw them together pretty much 24/7. That *could* work out well. Or it could cause problems.

He got up from the patio, went back inside to his computer, hit the reply button, and wrote:

"Of course you can come and visit. Mi tiempo es su tiempo, y asimismo mi templo es su templo. There are no hotels in Villa Rosario, but you are welcome to stay with me. My bed is big, and I don't snore. Just let me know."

That should do it, he thought, as he hit the send button. Carolina's Spanish was fairly good, and he hoped that she appreciated the pun he had written in Spanish: *my time is your time, and likewise my temple is your temple.* And it was true that there were no hotels in Villa Rosario, and the ones up in La Chorrera were not particularly great and were thirty to forty minutes away by bus. If she wanted to come and visit him, she would have to stay with him, and to stay with him meant they would have to share the same bed, because one bed was all he had in his small temple of a studio apartment.

He glanced around his place. He tried visualizing Carolina standing in his kitchen, or sitting out on his balcony, but mostly he tried visualizing her in his bed. What he had written about not snoring was probably not true, but he didn't want to dissuade her. He shook his head. Funny, he thought, how quickly a man will reposition his thoughts and behavior if there appears even the most remote chance to have sex with a woman. After years of being resigned to having Carolina as simply a friend, and after being her friend, he had immediately starting thinking about sex with her simply because of the possibility of her staying with him. Men, he thought... we're just so consumed by sex.

Or maybe it was just him.

His computer made that dinging tone, indicating another email. It was Carolina's reply:

"Thank you! It will be good to see you. I'll let you know the exact dates when I get tickets."

"Great", he emailed back. He smiled inwardly to see that she avoided any comment about the bed. Keeping her options open, he thought. Smart girl.

Later that night he was Skyping with Marta. Because of his history with Marta, she was his complete confidant. They held no secrets with each other. He had always thought they were like two soldiers who had served together in the same hellish war, fighting side by side, sleeping in the muddy trenches together, binding each other's wounds, saving each other's lives. Thus, he had, of course, told her everything about Marco and their lovemaking at the Hotel de Sevilla, and had just finished explaining to her about Carolina's email, his response, and his secret hopes.

"Well, you know, Ricardo," Marta was saying, "I'm not sure you should get your hopes up too high. It sounds like she's coming to Panama not so much to see you, as to get away from her job. Do you think she would have asked to visit you if her job had been going well?"

"Probably not," Ricardo had to admit. "Still, Marta, a man can hope."

"Does she know about Marco?" Marta asked.

"Well, not in any detail. I mean, she's always known I'm bisexual and she knows about Marco, but I've never told her that Marco and I had sex. But she's a bright girl. I would think she would have figured that out."

"And does Marco know about her?"

"I haven't talked with Marco today. He's working all this week. But he knows about her, yes. I've shown him pictures of her on my cell phone. He thinks she's cute."

Marta laughed. "You're thinking of trying to do a

threesome, aren't you?"

"Well, " Ricardo replied, "the thought did cross my mind, but I doubt if that'll happen. I could talk Marco into it, but I don't think Carolina would go for it. I'd have better luck if I could find another girl to bring to bed with Carolina. She's bisexual too, you know."

"I remember that," Marta said. "Is she seeing anyone right now?"

"You know... I don't know," Ricardo said. "She hasn't mentioned anyone, but I didn't ask, either this afternoon when she emailed me, or when I saw her for dinner during my trip."

"You should find out," Marta said.

"Yeah, I should... I should." Ricardo paused, and then said, "But you're probably right. It might end up being two weeks of asexual sleeping together... but it's going to be impossible for me to lie next to her and not want to touch her."

"Ha," said Marta. "Well, it'll be an interesting predicament. Maybe it'll turn into the fling you said you wanted."

"Um, no," Ricardo replied. "I can't imagine Carolina falling madly in love with me... She's too independent."

"And you're *not*?" Marta teased.

"Yeah, well... *I've* fallen madly in love before, so I know I'm capable of it. But I don't think Carolina ever has. She's never talked about love that way."

Later that night, after his Skype session with Marta, Ricardo was sitting on his little balcony patio having a glass of Sangría and thinking about Carolina, about his conversation with Marta, and about love. What he had said to Marta was true. He had fallen in love, several times, deep mad passionate love. But it had always seemed to lead to disastrous results. Two divorces, more broken hearts, and a type of pain that never seemed to go away. He had suffered. Worse, he had caused other people—women he had cared about—to suffer. Some mistakes, he had always thought, cannot be forgiven. Consequently, either by choice or by simply growing older, he had learned to hold back. He patronized brothels and bathhouses to take care of his sexual needs, which almost eliminated the possibility of finding another prospective long-term partner. He had to think back to when he had last felt that "swept-away" feeling of being in helplessly in love. It had been at least ten years or more. Why was it then, he wondered, that he wanted that experience again now? If falling in love always ends in hopeless pain and suffering, why did he want to do it again? He smiled to himself when the answer occurred to him.

He wanted to do it again because it made the sex so good.

Chapter 5:   The Brujo

That night Ricardo dreamed again. He dreamed that he had taken a bus from Villa Rosario, and had fallen asleep on the bus. When he awoke, he was no longer on the bus but standing in the middle of a huge, but unknown, bus station. There were hundreds of people walking in and out of the station, getting onto buses, or getting off buses. But none of the people looked at him—they were all preoccupied with their own destinations. None of the buses had any names on the front indicating where they were going. Ricardo tried to ask someone where he was, but no one spoke either English or Spanish. So he just continued walking back and forth in the bus station while dozens of buses came and went. He looked at each bus trying to find a sign to someplace familiar, or a face that looked friendly.

Finally, he looked down the way to the exit door, twenty feet from where all the passengers were walking. Standing there, in front of the exit door, was the brujo. He was wearing a long coat, like a trench coat, but Ricardo could somehow see through it, and there was that electric blue semen swirling around his testicles and pulsating in time with every beat of the brujo's heart. And this time Ricardo could make out the brujo's cock. It hung large and heavy, surrounded by thick pubic hair, illuminated by the soft pulsating glow of the blue semen from his scrotum. The brujo was stocky, with dark skin and short white hair and a white mustache. He was holding something in each hand. It looked to Ricardo that there was a knife in his right hand and something like the top spiky portion of a pineapple in his left hand. Pineapple juice was dripping from the severed top to the floor. None of the passengers seemed to notice the brujo. They all just walked right past him. But Ricardo stood there staring at him, afraid to step any closer. There was something ominous, something wrong. Ricardo was wanting to get away, but the only exit out of the bus station was the exit door right behind where the brujo was standing.

Ricardo woke up suddenly. His bedroom was very dark. He checked the clock by the bed. 2:30 in the morning. He shuddered involuntarily and pulled the thin blanket up closer. He was starting to hate this brujo dream. He tried to make out objects in the room, to reassure himself that he was awake and in his own bedroom. There was the stucco wall, its whiteness a rough dark gray in the blackness of night; there was the sound of the wind outside; there was his little writing desk, and his chair with yesterday's clothes strewn over the back. Just then the refrigerator compressor kicked on. Everything seemed in its place. Ricardo threw the covers off him and got up to pee.

*   *   *

Ricardo finally was able to fall back to sleep, and slept until mid-morning. That afternoon, he had lunch with Dan. Dan was a retired LA cop that Ricardo had met at Ted's apartment building when Ricardo first moved to Villa Rosario six years ago. Dan's past life in law enforcement had always been a little bit sketchy to Ricardo, but he had become a good friend, so Ricardo never probed. This was their first get-together since Ricardo had gotten back from his trip to the States.

"You look a little tired," Dan had said when he first sat down at the café. "Are you still feeling the effects of jet lag?"

"No," Ricardo replied. "Actually, it was an easy flight back. I just didn't sleep well last night."

"Down at Jenny's?" Dan teased.

"Ha, no, I wish. No, just bad dreams."

"Ah yes," Dan said, "bad dreams, the sign of a clean

conscience."

"Ha. No, for some reason lately, I've been having this recurring dream, where this brujo dude keeps showing up. Last night he was carrying a knife. At first, I thought he had a pineapple top in his hand, but later when I started thinking about it, it might have been a human scalp. I don't know. Woke me up at about two a.m., and it took me hours to fall back to sleep."

"Hmmm," Dan said and picked up the menu. "You know, we have one of those here in town."

"One of what?"

"A witch-doctor, a brujo. Lives up in the hills. Nobody talks about him and everyone leaves him alone."

"Really? What does he look like?" Ricardo asked.

"Don't know. I've never seen him. The only reason I even know about him is that don Fernando doesn't like him. Whenever someone disappears, he always wants to pin it on this brujo, but he never can."

"What? Who's don Fernando?" Ricardo asked.

"You remember him," Dan said, "the chief of police here."

"I thought his name was José Fernando."

"Well, it is. But all the locals refer to him as don Fernando, out of respect. So I've fallen into that habit too."

"Oh, right, okay."

Ricardo remembered José Fernando. Not only was he the local police chief, but he seemed to be Dan's best friend. Dan had introduced Ricardo to him years ago when there had been a series of murders in Villa Rosario and one of the victims had lived in Ted's apartment building.

"Anyway, back to this brujo guy," Ricardo said. "Is he real? I mean, is he a *real* brujo? Potions and magic and stuff?"

Dan put his menu down and looked at Ricardo. "I don't know. I really don't know anything about him except that he lives somewhere up in the hills nearby. But it's no big deal, you know. Those people have always existed in Central and South America. It's part of their culture, going back, well, probably going back to the stone age. I mean, someone's got to be the medicine man in any tribe. Someone's got to keep track of which plants will kill you and which make you feel better. Someone's got to dispense advice to people. And even though Panama's got modern pharmacies and medical clinics, those old habits don't die. You go take a look at the pharmacy here in town, or any pharmacy in Panama for that matter. You'll see hundreds of herbal medicines that just don't exist in the States, and you'll see the pharmacist still recommending them over any of our modern medicines. It's just part of the culture down here."

"Hmmm... Well, why doesn't José Fernando like this guy?"

"Probably some old family feud. Those old brujos are a law among themselves. They have no regard for authority. And you know don Fernando—he thinks he's on a mission from God to instill law and order."

The waitress came by to take their order. Afterwards, Dan picked up the conversation. "You know, down here it's easy to disappear. For example, a local girl just meet some boy from Colombia, fall in love and run away with him—just up and move to Colombia. And if she can't write, there's no letters home, or even if she can, the postal system doesn't work, and only a few cities have internet and none of the locals have a computer, so her family never hears from her again. And once she gets pregnant, she'll stay wherever she is and just raise babies. Happens all the time. The young people in this town have nothing, so they'll leave for any reason that looks like a better opportunity. But that kind of thing drives don Fernando crazy. Parents come to him wanting to know where their daughter is, and he can't help them, so he looks for someone to blame. Brujos are a great scapegoat for any mystery. I know one old guy here, for example, his father passed away about three years ago. I happened to ask him, without thinking really, how his father died, and he replied matter-of-factly that the brujo had put a spell on him and killed him. In many ways, it's still the Middle Ages down here. If you don't know anything about disease, it's easy to blame a witch. The difference is, in the Middle Ages, they'd just burn a witch. But here, people are really afraid of this guy.

He's untouchable. I bet even if don Fernando had evidence of him doing a crime, ultimately even don Fernando would back down. This brujo's not a curandero or a chamán, you know."

"No, I don't know," Ricardo replied. "What are those?"

"Well, there are different kinds of brujos. The chamanes and the cujanderos are indigenous natives, Indians who live way up in the hills and uses plants for healing other tribal members, the equivalent to medicine men. They're okay. The espiritistas can be indigenous or Panamanian, and they just talk to spirits and give advice; they don't usually mess with plants. Most of them are frauds, but they do no real harm. And the brujos can likewise be indigenous or Panamanian, but they do magic, cast spells, etc., and they can be either *brujos de mágico blanco* or *brujos de mágico negro*, and people here fear the latter."

"And this guy?" Ricardo asked.

"Oh, he's a *brujo de mágico negro*."

"And does he really do black magic?"

"Who knows?," Dan replied. "People are so superstitious down here that his reputation alone is enough to keep people away. But like I say, I've never seen him. He never comes to town, and I really don't know much about him. Hell, he may have died years ago. These kinds of myths live a long time. To me, it's all kind of bullshit."

"Well, do me a favor Dan," Ricardo said, "ask your don Fernando about him. I'm kind of curious."

"Sure."

Chapter 6:   Leslie

Ever since his Skype conversation with Marta, Ricardo had it in mind to find out if Carolina was seeing anyone, as that might make a difference in terms of his chances of having sex with her. That is, if in fact she came to visit him. It had been several days since her email, and he had not heard more from her. So the next evening, he sat down at his laptop and searched through Facebook until he found her page, and then he texted her.

"Any news on the airline ticket front?" he typed.

A few minutes later, she texted back, "No, I still need to do that. It's on my list for tomorrow."

He wondered why she hadn't done it yet, but only typed, "Okay, just let me know."

The thing he hated about Facebook, Twitter, and texting in general was how the communication always felt so curt. There was never any background information, never any explanation or description, never any emotion. It all felt so military and to the point. The medium forced that style of communication. But everyone used text messaging. Regular conversation was going the way of the handwritten postal letter. To get any context or background information out of someone via text, one almost had to interrogate them. So he decided to press Carolina a bit.

"How's the witch hunt going?" he wrote.

"They're still reviewing my curriculum," she replied. "They haven't interviewed anyone yet."

"I see," he typed. "Still think it'll take all semester?"

"Yeah, I hate it."

"Sorry," he wrote. "I know it's stressful."

"It's killing me," she typed back.

"Well, now's the time to gather your friends around you for support."

"I wish I could," she wrote.

He typed a lone question mark, then added, "Why can't you?"

"Leslie and I are breaking up. Most of my friends are her friends, too."

Ricardo leaned in towards the computer screen and re-read her last text. Who the fuck was Leslie? Was this Leslie a guy or a girl? Why hadn't she mentioned Leslie at the dinner they had just a few short weeks earlier?

"Do I know Leslie?" he typed.

"I don't think so. She moved in with me when I got to the university six weeks ago. She's a graduate student over in Engineering."

"Just roommates?" he typed, "Or more?"

"Well, it was more, but just roommates now. We barely talk. She wants to move out. This week has been hell. Work is horrible, and then I have to come home to her not talking to me."

Ricardo shook his head. So, she had started an affair with a graduate student as soon as she got to the university. Shit. Even though Leslie was in an entirely different department, she was still a student at the same university. Ricardo didn't want to ask Carolina what she was thinking when she did that, so he just typed, "I'm sorry." After a pause, he added, "Is she in any way connected with this investigation?"

"No, not that I know of," came the reply.

Ricardo didn't know what else to write. He just sat here trying to take this new information in. Was this the real reason Carolina wanted to get away for spring break? But then Carolina typed, "Maybe the whole PhD thing was a mistake."

"No, no," he quickly typed back. "A doctorate can open up all kinds of doors. Remember how bad it was working for the state, when you just had an MSW?"

"This is just as stressful," she wrote.

"Look, you've just hit a patch of politics. There's politics everywhere. Hang in there; you'll weather this."

"I just feel like quitting. It's all just such bullshit. I'm so done with working for other people, and with relationships."

"Well, my dear, work and love are the only two things that make life worthwhile."

"There's traveling," she typed. "I just want to travel and see the world."

Ricardo recalled that one of the reasons Carolina was eager to work in academia was so she could have her summers off to travel. He typed back, "You'll get through this, and you'll be able to travel this summer."

"I hope so," she wrote.

This back-and-forth exchange went on for another thirty minutes. She seemed reluctant to say more about Leslie, and Ricardo didn't want to pry too much. It was obvious to Ricardo that Carolina was more deeply distraught and unhappy than he had thought. The only encouraging information was that she had gotten back into therapy and had an appointment the next day. That was a good sign, he thought, and he praised her for doing that. At the end of their texting session, she apologized for being so negative, and thanked him for being her friend. They said their goodbyes with a promise to text or talk again soon.

Ricardo sat back and thought some more. He simply did not know what to make of this new information. He decided to open a bottle of Sangría and go sit out on his porch and think about it. But first, since he was already logged on to Facebook, he decided to search for Marco. He did a quick search and found Marco's page. And he saw that Marco had posted a slew of photographs of himself with friends at the Playa Caimito. Playa Caimito was a rocky beach near La Chorrera, not particularly pretty but popular because it was easy to get to from Villa Rosario. Ricardo looked at the posting and the comments. Evidently Marco had been there all day today. The friends were all young men, Marco's age. They were laughing, splashing in the water, and playing on the rocks near the beach.

The problem was that when he and Marco had returned to Villa Rosario from the Hotel de Sevilla, Marco had told him that the restaurant had scheduled him to work the next six days. Ricardo had assumed that was why he hadn't heard from Marco that week. Yet here he was, obviously at the beach and not waiting tables. It was none of Ricardo's concern, except that... except that he felt somehow shut out.

Ricardo turned his laptop off, went into the kitchen, opened a bottle of Sangría, poured himself a large glass over ice, and went out on the patio to think.

The sky was black, but the stars were bright, and the air was cool. He sat there on his little patio chair, just sipping Sangría, and thinking.

Am I just out of the loop? he wondered to himself. Both Carolina and Marco were more than half his age. Maybe that's what all young people do: act without thinking about consequences. Maybe he was just seeing both of their actions through an older man's eyes. He would never take a lover at a place where he worked, absolutely never... but then he thought back to when he was in his thirties, and he remembered that he had done exactly that. Not only did the woman work at the job with him, she was his direct subordinate... and she was married! Yet they had carried on an affair for six months, all out of sight of the other workers and her husband. Such an affair would be grounds for a lawsuit and dismissal these days, but decades ago... well, decades ago he had been younger. Times were different, true, but the main difference was that he had been much younger and never considered the implications of his actions. How was that any different from what Carolina was doing? She was just being young and stupid, just as he had been young and stupid. And maybe that was the same with Marco. If Ricardo had just returned from a two-day romantic and sexual tryst with someone, he would have kept in touch with them and explained that he was taking a day off and going to the beach with friends. He would have naturally done that out of courtesy—to avoid any potential jealous feelings, and simply to share what he was doing. But thinking back again to his own thirties, he had to admit he had never been transparent with anyone back then. Almost everything he had said back then was a calculated lie, either of omission or commission. So, like Carolina, maybe Marco was simply being young too, simply omitting to tell Ricardo about going to the beach with his friends because it was easier than bringing it up... maybe... maybe.

But maybe, Ricardo thought, *he* was the one who was being blind and foolish. Maybe Marco had slept with him in return for a free trip to a fancy resort, an air-conditioned room, a great beach, and wonderful meals. Maybe Carolina just considered him an old man who cared about her... a father figure... a father figure who was perhaps older than her actual father. Maybe the idea of him as a lover never crossed her mind, or worse, was repugnant to her, so she had put up with his flirting and light advances over the years simply in exchange for his friendship, support, and advice.

Ricardo's thoughts turned darker. The idea that Marco had just let him use his body, suck that thick cock, and kiss those lips, only because Ricardo had had the money to pay for the Hotel de Sevilla, disturbed Ricardo. He tried to rationalize it, the same way he had before the trip to the hotel, telling himself that seduction always involved a difference in resources. But this time logic could not overcome his feelings of being both used and being a user.

Worse, he knew he would never find out the truth. We never really can know the truth about other people, he thought. If Carolina slept with him, would it be out of pity and/or desperation, or would it be because she really liked him? If she didn't sleep with him, would it mean she was turned off by him, or would it be because she was distraught about breaking up with Leslie and worried about her job? Or would it mean that she had stopped feeling bisexual and was only feeling attracted to women these days? And the same dilemma was true with Marco. If Marco slept with him again, would it be because Ricardo was paying for his meals, or because he actually *liked* Ricardo? He would never know, never know for sure.

He wondered if that's how it always is for humans. Maybe we simply never know how the other thinks of us. *The other*, Ricardo thought. And even if the other likes us this week, this month, or this year, there is no guarantee that he or she will feel the same in the future. Always the deception, always the misrepresentation, always the presentation... If a person was good-looking, pleasant, and artful, they could charm your life savings away. If it wasn't for the sex, the physical contact, the caresses, and feeling of being loved, he wouldn't want anything to do with other people, Ricardo thought. He was an idiot, a fool because of his own longing for others, his own weakness for the contact of naked human flesh.

He went back inside and refilled his glass with Sangría. He couldn't stop wondering if he was being used by both Carolina and Marco. It was going to be a troublesome night. Once the monkey-chatter of doubt and recrimination inside his brain got started, the only way he could drown it out was by drinking.

Chapter 7: Jenny's

The next day started off rough. Ricardo had not slept well the night before. He woke up thinking he had dreamt again about the brujo, but it was just a feeling. He couldn't remember any images. But he knew he had tossed and turned, feeling off-kilter with both Marco and Carolina. He had decided to not contact Carolina for a day or two, to see if she actually did make airplane reservations to come see him. He did, however, send Marco a short email after breakfast, inquiring how he was doing and mentioning the possibility of getting together for lunch sometime soon.

After more coffee, he sat down at his writing desk and turned his attention to one of the only two things in life that ever brought him peace—writing. "Work," he thought to himself, "the great narcotic." He wrote all morning, skipped lunch, and by early afternoon had finished that short story about Cindy and her new lover Sarah and her now ex-lover Dave. When it was finally done, he proofread it several times, not only for spelling and grammar, but also for continuity, flow, and believability. Ricardo always proofread out loud so he could hear the way the words fit together, like stepping stones in a garden, leading the reader somewhere. Finally, he stood up and stretched. His back was aching from so many hours sitting, but he had a very pleasing sense of accomplishment. He liked the story. Most of his stories, he had noticed over the years, were dark, and the characters always doomed by some flaw. But in this one, Cindy actually grew as a person, actually made choices that were healthy for her, and ended up a stronger person. Not his normal style, Ricardo thought, but satisfying nonetheless. He sat back down and emailed the story to his publisher with a small note. Even if his publisher didn't like that the story had a relatively happy ending, Ricardo knew that there was enough sex in the story to make the publisher include it in the next book of short stories.

Ricardo felt lucky to have such a good arrangement with his publisher. Whenever Ricardo finished a short story, he would simply email it in. When the publisher felt he had enough material for another book, he would contact Ricardo. They would discuss the book title and the order of the stories, and the book would be published. Ricardo trusted his publisher's judgment, and left the marketing details to him. Besides, auditing his royalty statements was his tax accountant's job. Ricardo just wanted to be left alone to write. He didn't make a lot of money from the books, but it was steady. That money plus his Social Security was enough to let him live, not extravagantly, but comfortably, in Villa Rosario. It would not have been enough to live on in the States, but it was enough for Panama—enough for him to afford occasional retreats to places like Hotel de Sevilla, visits to the bathhouses of La Chorrera, and occasional trips to Jenny's.

Ricardo made himself some lunch and sat out on his little balcony to eat. *Jenny's,* he thought. *Maybe I'll go there tonight.* He watched the little yellow birds chasing bugs in the air. He watched the palm trees sway. He watched the soft white clouds drift over the central valley below. He thought about Jenny and her little brothel. The sex was always good there. Sex was the only other thing that brought him peace. *Sex and writing,* he thought, *thank God for both.* Once again, he thought about how lucky he was. Not only did he love living in Villa Rosario, but he was just a short bus ride to what he thought was the nicest, safest brothel he had ever been to.

He took his plate and glass back inside to the kitchen to wash them. After cleaning up, Ricardo lay down in his bed. It had turned out to be a good day, and now the late lunch had made him sleepy. He closed his eyes and was soon asleep... deep asleep.

And this time he did dream about the brujo.

He was in bed somewhere other than his apartment. He was in bed fucking some woman. He was on top, thrusting away. They were both sweaty. Their naked bodies made a wet slapping sound as they smacked against each other. He looked down to see who the woman was. It was Carolina, only it wasn't Carolina. He was fucking her harder and harder. He looked up. There was the brujo, coming towards the bed. His pants were undone and his cock was out, semi-erect and getting harder. The blue semen had filled his scrotum and was wanting to burst out. The brujo was just staring at Ricardo, but Ricardo knew that the brujo wanted him to take his cock in his mouth and suck it—to suck it and gag on all that semen. The brujo was closer now. Ricardo didn't want to do this. The brujo's cock was large and now erect, the foreskin pulled away from the head. The cock was dark, darker than the brujo, and Ricardo could smell it—it had a gamy smell, like he hadn't washed in weeks. Ricardo looked down at Carolina—she had stopped moving. He looked closer. She was dead. She had been dead for quite a while. He was fucking a corpse. The brujo's cock was inches from Ricardo's mouth. The brujo reached out with both hands to grab Ricardo's head.

When Ricardo awoke, it was dark outside. He must have slept for hours. His body ached. He felt sick. He hated these kinds of bad dreams. He rubbed his eyes and reached over to the table and looked at the clock. It was almost 6:30 p.m. He had slept for almost four hours! He got up, stumbled into the bathroom and splashed cold water on this face.

He dried his face, stepped out of the bathroom and turned on all the lights in his tiny apartment. Even though it was night, Ricardo poured a half cup of left-over cold coffee from the coffee pot into a cup and heated it in the microwave. Though it was bitter, he wanted a few sips because he still felt groggy from such a deep sleep. As he sipped at the coffee he thought how that dream had ruined a good day. It made him mad that a stupid dream could intrude on his paradise and darken his mood. He tried to shake it off. He had had different kinds of submission/domination dreams before, he told himself. This was just another one of those.

He opened the apartment door to see how cool the evening was. A nice breeze blew through the doorway. He changed from his shorts into long pants and a shirt, made sure he had his wallet with some money in it, and headed down to the Parque Central to catch a bus to La Chorrera to go to Jenny's.

The cool night air and the walk downtown made Ricardo feel better. Or perhaps it was just the caffeine waking him from his stupor. During the bus ride he actually started anticipating sex at Jenny's. He wondered who Jenny would pick for him.

Jenny's brothel was different from other brothels, and Jenny was different than any other madam. There was no line-up of girls. In fact, no girls were present in the main room when you walked in. There was just Jenny. She would talk to you for a while, about who you were, where you were from, and how you were feeling that night, and then she would select a girl for you. She would call one of her workers and they would come downstairs and Jenny would introduce you. If you did not like the girl, that was it. You had to leave. There were no other choices, no other options for you that night. But if you liked the girl, (and Jenny's selection was usually spot on), you could go upstairs with her and negotiate price. If some other client came to the door while Jenny was talking to you, she made them go away for twenty minutes or so, so she could finish interviewing you. If clients showed up drunk, or even if Jenny didn't like the way they looked, they couldn't come in. Jenny was no-nonsense and ran the brothel her way. And Ricardo knew that she always packed a small pistol if she needed to make a point with a wayward customer. Plus, she ran a clean brothel. Condoms were required, and the girls were checked by a nurse each week for STDs. Prices were high, but Ricardo thought it was well worth it.

Over the years, he and Jenny had become friends, of sorts—as much of a friendship that might exist between a madam and a favorite customer. Jenny's husband was Ted, the gringo landlord from whom Ricardo rented his first apartment years ago in Villa Rosario. And Jenny had encouraged a relationship, also years ago now, between Ricardo and Magali, one of Jenny's sex workers. He and Magali had lived together for a while, but eventually, as with all of Ricardo's relationships, they split up. Magali continued to work for Jenny for almost a year after their break-up, but Jenny always kept her out of sight when Ricardo came over. Eventually Magali had moved on, Jenny had told him, first to Panama City, and then somewhere else.

But that was years ago, and Ricardo was not thinking of Magali tonight when he pushed the buzzer on Jenny's door.

After a minute, Jenny opened it. "Ah, don Ricardo. Pase, pase!"

Ricardo stepped inside saying, "Gracias, Jenny. ¿Cómo estás?

"I am well, don Ricardo," Jenny said in Spanish and stood there looking him over. Ricardo thought he saw a tiny frown cross her forehead. "Come in and have a seat. Would you like some tea?"

"Yes, thank you, that would be lovely."

Jenny only served tea at her brothel—no coffee, no soft drinks, and definitely no alcohol.

She brought Ricardo a cup of tea, with two lumps of sugar already stirred into it, just how he liked it. Then she sat down on the couch across from him.

"I'm afraid, don Ricardo, that I may not have anyone for you tonight. I know what you like, but no one here tonight would be a good fit for you. I have a new girl coming back tomorrow. I have interviewed her, and the nurse has taken blood samples. And yesterday she saw my doctor for a physical. You know I love my girls, but I always test them. They complain that the nurse sticks them with so many needles each week that they are like pincushions. But I will have all her test results back by tomorrow morning when she is coming in for me to talk with her one more time. I think you might like her, but first I must make sure she is totally clean.

Ricardo was disappointed. This happened occasionally, but not often, and he had not factored it into his vision of tonight. "Oh dear, Jenny, well I am sorry too."

"I tell you what don Ricardo, I like this new girl—I think she would be a good match for you. If she is clean, I will call you at your house tomorrow, and you can be the first client to meet her."

"Well, Jenny, that would be an honor. Thank you so much."

"We have been friends a long time, don Ricardo. I treat you as a son."

Ricardo just smiled. What an image, he thought to himself, a mother who arranges her own son's hookers. How good is that?

"You know, don Ricardo, I interviewed someone else last week. I did not take her, but I thought of you. She was a... a he."

"Un travesti?" Ricardo asked, using the word for transvestite.

"No, more than that," Jenny said, "she was a woman on top but a man down below. I did not believe her. I thought she was all woman, so I made her show me. And down below, she was a bull... well, more like a billy goat." Jenny laughed, then continued. "She explained that she had surgery in Columbia. It was very good. I could hardly see any scars. Anyway, I thought you might like that. But I knew it would freak out the rest of my clients, so I didn't hire her. There's not enough diversity of tastes here in La Chorrera. She might find work in Panama City."

"I'm sure she will," Ricardo said.

Jenny's intuition always fascinated Ricardo. It was what made her so good as a matchmaker. Jenny's "interviews" with clients never probed into their sexual tastes. He certainly had never said a word to her about his own sexual preferences, and yet Ricardo knew that at some level Jenny knew all about him. He thought of her as a *sensitive*, an old New York term for someone who was naturally psychic about someone. In another culture, she would have been an excellent marriage matchmaker, he thought. She was kind, chatty, with an almost old lady-like charm. But underneath that exterior, she was deadly accurate about people.

They talked about other things for a while: weather, local politics, and the tribulations of running a brothel. Then that little frown crossed Jenny's face again, and she said, "But I must ask, don Ricardo. You look troubled... Is everything okay?

"Yeah," he replied, "everything is good. I just haven't been sleeping well lately."

She looked at him. That little frown became bigger. "Bad dreams?"

"Uh huh."

"Dreams about a brujo, perhaps?" she asked.

He felt a sudden tightening in the pit of his stomach. This was way beyond simply being intuitive.

"Yes, but... but how did you know?"

"Oh, he's been everywhere lately, in many people's dreams. He's hunting."

"Hunting?" Ricardo exclaimed, "What do you mean?"

"When a brujo needs a new victim, he searches them out in their dreams," she said. "He usually prefers young women, but he will take men of a certain... a certain persuasion. He comes to them in their dreams, and tries to seduce them, tries to make them want to come to him."

"And then what happens?"

"Well," Jenny replied, "No one knows. If they go to him, they disappear. We never see them again."

"Wait a minute, wait a minute, Jenny. Let's back up. You're talking about the brujo of Villa Rosario? He's really a real person?"

"Oh yes, don Ricardo. Yes...at least, he *was* a real person. He has not been seen in over fifteen years, not since don Fernando burned his house down in Villa Rosario. That was right before I came to La Chorrera. But it is why the people of Villa Rosario keep don Fernando as the police chief. He burned the brujo's house down, and the brujo fled to the hills. So they made don Fernando the police chief because he was the only one to stand up to the brujo... well, him and Padre Lopez. Between me and you, I think it was Padre Lopez who actually lit the fire, but he asked don Fernando to take the credit because it would not look right for a priest to do such an act of violence."

Ricardo had heard of Father Lopez, the retired priest who lived in a small house behind the Church at the Parque Central of Villa Rosario. He was very old, white-haired, and stooped over. Ricardo had even seen him once or twice, sitting in the park. But he had never spoken to him.

Jenny stood up, looked at Ricardo's cup and asked, "More tea, don Ricardo?" Ricardo just nodded his head. Jenny took Ricardo's cup and took it to a sideboard where the teapot sat on a hotplate. She poured the tea, added two lumps of sugar, stirred it, and returned to Ricardo, placing the full cup on the table next to him. Ricardo was barely aware of her having done this, but the rattling of the cup as she set it down brought him back from his spinning thoughts.

"Jenny, what does this brujo look like?" he asked.

"I don't know, don Ricardo, I have never seen him."

"What do people say he looks like?"

"Well, I had a girl working for me a few years ago, the last time he was on a hunt. She saw him in her dreams..."

"Wait a minute," Ricardo interrupted. "Exactly what is this hunt, and how do you know he's on one now?"

"Well, Villa Rosario, and even La Chorrera, are small towns, don Ricardo, when people start having the same dream, word gets around. All the parents get very nervous— they don't want to lose their little girls, so they all hammer crucifixes and ajo plants above their daughters' beds."

"Crosses and garlic?" exclaimed Ricardo.

"Well, they *are* peasants, don Ricardo. What do you expect? They see that in the movies and they think it works. But Padre Lopez told me that it's useless against the brujo. Odd isn't it? A priest admitting that the crucifix is powerless?"

"So how often does he hunt?"

"Once every three or four years this happens. It goes on for about a month, then it suddenly stops. Sometimes someone disappears and it stops, but other times it just stops. But when it stops, the townspeople all assume that he has taken someone."

Ricardo just sat there shaking his head. "You started to say, before I interrupted you... you started to say that one of your girls had dreams about him. When was that?"

"About four years ago, the last time he was hunting. Yes, this girl worked for me and she started having terrible dreams about the brujo. She got scared and went back to live with her parents in Santiago. She was safe there because the brujo will not hunt far from this area."

"And what did she say he looked like? I mean, in her dreams?" Ricardo asked.

"Hmmm, I think she said he was short, white hair, nothing unusual that I can remember, a typical older Panameño."

"Did she say anything else about him?"

"Well, she implied the dreams were very sexual."

"Did she say if he had a mustache?" Ricardo asked.

"I don't remember anything like that. But it's been four years... Drink your tea don Ricardo It will get cold."

"Oh yes. Thank you, Jenny."

They sat there in silence for a few minutes, Ricardo sipping his tea trying to gather his thoughts, and Jenny sitting patiently, looking at him.

Short with white hair... well, Jenny was right. That would describe about ninety-five percent of older Panamanian men. Ricardo tried to be rational. A whole town getting scared because some people had bad dreams? He knew enough about crowd hysteria to know how quickly rumors can spread through a community. As for the people of Villa Rosario, as much as Ricardo loved them, Jenny was not wrong in calling them peasants. Few of them had ever gone to high school. They farmed the nearby fields, raised a few cows, and sold produce at the local open-air markets. He was probably getting worked up over nothing, falling into the same superstitious hysteria. But he couldn't deny that he did feel a bit scared. He had been having dreams about a brujo; he had identified him as a brujo before his conversation with Dan, before he had even learned there was a brujo in this area; and Jenny had guessed that he was having those dreams...

"Don Ricardo," Jenny said, interrupting his thoughts, "do not worry. I am sorry I even brought it up. These are just bad dreams. You are safe from the brujo. He cannot take you."

"Why do you say that?"

"Because a brujo cannot just take someone. The person must choose to go to the brujo."

"Then why the dreams?" Ricardo asked.

"That's how brujos work. They invade people's dreams, looking for someone who wants to come to him. If the person does not go, soon the dreams stop, and the brujo goes in search of someone else."

Ricardo had somehow assumed that the aim of the brujo's hunt was to kill people, but Jenny seemed to be saying something else.

"Why would someone want to go to a brujo?" he asked.

Jenny looked a bit sad. "We are a poor people. Especially the young. They think that if they join up with a brujo, they will have power, wealth, respect. Those things are very seductive to the young."

"That girl who worked for you... was she tempted?"

"No, no, I don't think so. She only said that the dreams were very sexual, and they scared her. She packed up her things and left very quickly. More tea, don Ricardo?"

Ricardo looked at his watch, then said, "No, no thank you Jenny. I think I'll head back home. You have given me much to think about."

"I am sorry don Ricardo. Please, do not worry. You are safe. But if you want more information, you should talk to Padre Lopez in Villa Rosario. He knows more about the brujo than anyone else in this area. Tell him I sent you."

"Okay, I may do that. How do you know him, Jenny?"

Jenny smiled. "Well, in my line of work, I usually meet everyone... eventually."

Ricardo laughed for the first time that evening. "I bet

you do, Jenny, I bet you do. Well, good night, thank you for the tea. Let me know about the new girl."

"I won't forget, don Ricardo. Yes, I think she might be just the thing to take your mind off bad dreams. Good night."

On the bus ride back to Villa Rosario, Ricardo thought about all that Jenny had told him. He simply didn't know what to make of it. He only knew that the dreams about the brujo were frightening.

Otherwise, his life was normal.

The bus let him off at the bus stop at the Parque Central in Villa Rosario. The huge Catholic Church loomed over the park, as they do in most Panamanian towns. Ricardo glanced at it as he started to walk the few blocks to his apartment. He didn't think he would seek out Father Lopez, because he wasn't sure how to introduce himself. The idea of greeting him with "the madam of the local whorehouse sent me..." seemed a bit much.

That night Ricardo slept without dreams...at least, without any he could remember. He awoke the next morning feeling good, ready to face the world.

Chapter 8:   Alma

The next day, in the early afternoon, Ricardo's cell phone rang. It was Jenny.

"Hola, don Ricardo. I have Alma's test results back from the clinic."

"Who? What?"

"Alma! The new girl I told you about last night. She is clean. Would you like to meet her this evening, say around seven?"

Typical Jenny, Ricardo thought, Right to the point... All business. "Oh, yes, Jenny. Um, yes, that sounds good, yes, seven o'clock. I'll be there."

"Okay, see you then. Chau."

Yup... all Jenny. Make the appointment and we're done. Ricardo had the image of her sitting there with a list of clients to call. If Ricardo had said no, she would have just gone down to the next name. But at least his name was at the top of the list. He would make the bus trip back to La Chorrera again this evening... Okay, maybe this would be good. He always liked Jenny's choice of women for him. He had never been disappointed, and in a few cases, he had been amazed. He hoped Alma would be nice.

He returned to his writing desk where he had been working since early morning. He was playing with an idea for a new short story, drafting out sample paragraphs, thinking about characters, plot, and dialogue. He wasn't sure exactly what the story was about except that it involved a rock climber named Heath, a man who loved the outdoors and mountains. Against the advice of his family, he'd taken up free climbing—outdoor rock climbing without ropes or safety equipment. He was young and muscular, with extremely strong hands and fingers, and he loved the adrenaline and the exhilaration of going higher and higher up the sheer cliffs of mountains, knowing that one false move, one crumbling ledge, could send him to his death. His natural skill and enthusiasm had led him to early success and to the admiration of the local rock-climbing devotees, and thus he was spurned on to attempt even more dangerous mountains. In the story, he and some other rock climbers had traveled to the Idaho Falls area in search of new challenges. All Ricardo knew for sure is that the story would open with Heath waking up in his tent the first cold wet morning of the camping trip, getting up to make coffee, and to survey the mountain peaks that rose straight up near the base camp to the drizzly clouds above. And Ricardo knew how the story would end: with Heath falling to his death from the cliffs above, after making one stupid mistake. The events leading up to that stupid mistake would be recalled in a long flashback in Heath's mind as he was falling. But Ricardo was trying to determine what the actual mistake was. He was also trying to determine whether some girl was involved. Like most of his short stories, this one unfolded in his mind's eye as he sat at his computer. He could see Health standing in the cold damp morning, coffee cup in hand, staring upwards. And he could see some woman—a fellow climber—waking up in her tent and peeking out of her tent flaps to see Heath. Ricardo could make out her features, but he didn't know who she was, whether she would interact with Heath, or just be a silent observer. He did know that she would not make the climb that morning, that she possessed enough common sense to see that it was too drizzly and too cold to climb the rock face. But whether she tells Heath that, Ricardo just didn't know yet.

This was the way Ricardo had always written. These stories would come to him in one or two images, usually in the early morning as he was waking up. He would get out of bed, make coffee, go to his writing desk and just start transcribing them. If he came to a dead end, he would sit back, maybe rewind the image a bit, and let it play out a different way. He'd watch, then write, then stop and watch a bit more, then write, as if he were transcribing a movie. Often, at the end of a day or two, he'd have an interesting story. He'd re-read it a few times, and if he liked it, he would send it to his publisher, forget about it, and move on to transcribing the next movie that came along. Ricardo had no name for this type of writing—it was simply how he did it. Sometimes the story came fast, and he had to type as fast as he could. Other times, the movie would move slowly, scene by scene, and it took him hours to write one page.

Today was the latter case. The story was moving slowly, but nonetheless, Ricardo was intrigued. He liked the image and the feel of the wet gray mountain that faced Heath. It was almost as if the slick rock face had a smell: cold, hard, flinty. It almost smelled of gunpowder. Ricardo was curious how this story would develop.

But by mid-afternoon, a few hours after Jenny's call, Ricardo was tired. He never liked to push the stories. Four to six hours of writing a day, never more. He saved what he had written and shut down his computer. He checked his watch and counted the hours until 7:00. Then he decided to lie down for a short nap.

He fell asleep thinking about this new girl Alma. Jenny had not given him any indication what she looked like—she had only said that she thought he would like her. He slept well for about thirty minutes, then woke up feeling refreshed. He got up and made himself a little snack of reheated rice and salsa. He had skipped lunch, but it was too early for dinner. He never liked to go to Jenny's on a full stomach. He would catch dinner after Jenny's, on his way back home.

* * *

The bus ride to La Chorrera was uneventful, as was

69

the short walk from the bus stop to Jenny's. His mind seemed clear and free of thoughts. He knocked on the door; Jenny opened it and invited him in.

"Don Ricardo," she said in a theatrical voice, "how nice to see you again, so soon after just last night." Then she laughed. "Come in, come in. Have a seat and make yourself at home. I will get Alma." She picked up the phone on the table, dialed an internal extension, said something quiet, then hung up.

"She will be right down. I want you to... how do gringos say it?... knock yourself out tonight." She laughed again, then said, "Seriously, don Ricardo, this is Alma's first time here with me. I was on the fence about hiring her, because she is skinny and small-breasted. I know you like that, but most of my customers are Panameño. They like their women plump. But she came with good references and she claims she's very enthusiastic, very athletic. So I want you to try her out and then, in a day or two, give me your honest opinion of her. I can interview girls all day, but I do not know how they actually perform. You let me know, okay?"

"Will do, Jenny." Ricardo said, but he wondered to himself what kind of accessory to whoredom this made him: the official brothel test driver? Then Jenny added, mysteriously, "I'm trying to broaden my services." Ricardo was going to ask her what she meant by that, but just then Alma came down the stairs and into the room. Ricardo stood up to greet her and smiled. Jenny was right—Alma did look athletic. She was very slim, with small breasts, almost flat-chested, but he could tell she had muscles like a gymnast. She was wearing a simple long white sleeveless cotton smock that tied in the back. Her long black hair was also tied back and Ricardo could make out the muscle definition in her bare shoulders. Her skin color was very light coffee. Dark eyebrows, straight nose, and a wide friendly smile. Ricardo thought she was pretty.

"Alma, this is don Ricardo," Jenny said.

"Mucho gusto," said Alma.

"It's good to meet you," said Ricardo in Spanish.

"Why don't you two go upstairs and get to know each

other?" Jenny said. Alma took Ricardo by the hand and led him up the stairs.

Inside a room, they sat down on the bed, and Ricardo just looked at her. There was something about her face that he liked—it wasn't that she was a stunning beauty, but there was something—he couldn't quite put his finger on it, but there was something about her expression that made him feel at ease. Plus, she seemed to know what she was doing.

"You would like one hour, two hours or all night?"

"Two hours," Ricardo replied. Earlier that afternoon he had debated whether to stay all night, but he had decided that today he was more in the mood for sex and less for all-night cuddling. Besides, the price difference was substantial. But at Jenny's, he never took the one-hour option. One hour was fine for some brothels—in fact, in some brothels it was too much time—but the women at Jenny's were always too nice to only spend one hour with. He might not use the full two hours, but he never wanted to feel rushed.

He paid her, and she left the room to take the money to Jenny. Even though prostitution was legal in Panama, running a brothel was not, so Jenny never let any customer see her handle money. As far as the law was concerned, she just ran a small boarding house for women. What the women did up in their rooms was their own business. Plausible deniability.

While Alma was gone, Ricardo stripped down and took a quick shower in the glass shower stall that was part of the room. Jenny had designed her brothel so that each room had a built-in glass shower stall in the corner of the room, separate from the bathroom, which was off to one side. The shower-in-the-room had several advantages. The clients could shower and be clean for the girls while still keeping an eye on their clothes and wallet (not that Ricardo ever had a problem there). It encouraged the clients to shower before sex, which the girls appreciated, and it gave the girls a place to shower after sex, which the next client appreciated. Ricardo thought it was a brilliant feature.

Ricardo was just toweling himself dry when Alma came back into the room. She reached behind her back, undid the bow to her smock and slipped it over her head. Underneath she was completely naked. Ricardo stopped drying himself and just stared at her. She was extremely ripped, with tightly defined abdomen, leg and arm muscles. He didn't see an ounce of fat on her. Her breasts were small, but pointy, with long, almost black, nipples. A small dense patch of public hair covered her pussy. As she turned around to place her smock on a chair, he got to admire her butt—it was as firm as any Olympic swimmer's. She must work out, he thought to himself. He finished drying himself, noticing with disappointment his own soft white body.

Alma walked up to him, grabbed the towel out of his hand, and said, "I think you're dry enough." She tossed the towel onto the floor, grabbed both his shoulders, and backed him over to the bed. "Jenny told me you needed special attention—that I should take control of you." She pushed him up to edge of the bed—he could feel the mattress against the back of his knees. He reached up and placed both hands on her breasts, gently massaging the long nipples. She moved in closer, inches from him, and said, "You want me to be in control?" It was more of a statement than a question, but Ricardo looked into her brown eyes, inches from his. He could feel her breath.

"Yes," he said softly, "yes, I do."

She moved closer. He thought she was going to kiss him, but instead she stuck out her tongue and licked broadly across his mouth, leaving his lips and left cheek wet. Keeping her left hand on his right shoulder, she reached down with her right hand and took his cock in her hand, rasping his balls gently with her fingernails, and then pulling his cock towards her firmly and letting it fall away. She took her tongue, stuck it straight out, and poked the edges of his lips a few times, and repeated the stroke-and-release motion on his cock. He was starting to get hard. She laughed, and simply pushed him with her left hand so he fell back flat onto the bed. Then she climbed on top of him like a monkey. Ricardo could feel how strong she was. She maneuvered her climb so that her dense public hair pressed downward as she rubbed it over his cock and then up to his stomach. She reached up and grabbed both his arms by the wrists, pushed them out above his head, holding him down, and inched her way up until her face was level with his, just inches away.

"You want me to be in control?" she said again. "Yes," he repeated.

She smiled and said, "Then say it."

Suddenly Jenny's statement about expanding her services made sense to him. Alma was a Dom! Ricardo was getting very excited.

"Yes," he said, "I want you to be in control."

"And I can do whatever I want with your body?" she said.

"Yes."

"Say it," she demanded.

"You can do whatever you want with my body."

"Whatever I want."

"Whatever you want."

She continued to climb up his body and sat up on his chest, one knee on either side of his chest to support her. She released his wrists, then placed one knee after the other on either side of his head, raising herself up so her pelvis was several inches above his face, and said, "Then eat me," and began to lower her pussy onto his mouth. She leaned forward, extending her arms straight down to the bed to support her, and then buried her pussy in his face and began to move it back and forth.

Normally Ricardo would never do this with a prostitute, but he had given up all control by this point, and it would never have gotten to this point if he did not trust Jenny's disease testing procedures. He stuck his tongue out so that it went into Alma's wet pussy. She continued to move her pelvis back and forth so that her clit ran over his nose and back to his tongue. Pussy juices dripped down Ricardo's face, some into his nostrils, more into his mouth. He could feel the ruffled edges of her pussy lips as they glided firmly over his chin, his mouth, and his nose. He could feel the smooth slick fleshy walls inside her pussy with his tongue. Her taste was sweet, feminine, tangy, and exhilarating. He thrust his tongue out as hard as he could while gasping air into breath. Her dense pubic hair scratched the sides of his face. She pushed down harder and moved back and forth faster.

Her knees were positioned so that her shins and ankles held his shoulders down to the bed, but he was able to bend his arms and place both hands on her muscular thighs. She was all muscle. All muscle and all woman. He was so turned on that his cock was standing straight up even though neither she nor he was touching it.

Suddenly she laughed and fell off him, leaving him gasping for air to get his breath back. She ran two fingers into her pussy, pulled them out wet and stuck them into Ricardo's mouth. He licked and sucked them. She laughed again and jumped out of the bed and went over to the side table on the right of the bed and opened the top drawer, taking out a pair of handcuffs.

"Roll over," she commanded. Ricardo rolled to his left side facing her. She laughed and then said mockingly, "The other way, silly." He rolled over onto his right side, his erection sticking out. She grabbed his left arm and pulled it behind his back. "Give me your other arm," she said. He shoved his right arm underneath his side and behind him. She grabbed it, handcuffed his wrists together, and rolled him back onto his back. He shifted his locked hands up to the small of his back to get more comfortable.

Then she reached into the drawer and removed a large dildo. Ricardo stared at it. She held it out to show him, to watch his reaction, then she smiled. She took a condom from the drawer, sat down on the side of the bed, and holding the dildo between her knees, she unwrapped the condom and rolled it onto the dildo. She then grabbed a small jar from the drawer and stood up, looked at Ricardo, then went over and picked up the towel that she had thrown on the floor. Going over to Ricardo, she stuck one arm underneath both his knees and scooped up his legs from underneath, and with one arm lifted his legs up, which lifted half his torso up an inch over the bed. He was amazed at her strength. She spread the still-damp towel under his butt with her other hand and let his legs drop. Then she grabbed another condom from the drawer, opened it, and began to roll the condom onto Ricardo's cock. His cock had lost a bit of the erection, but she stroked it up and down a few times to get him hard again, and then continued rolling the condom down his shaft. Then she pushed his legs wide apart, grabbed the dildo, unscrewed the jar and started applying lubricant to the condom-covered dildo. Then she placed the wet dildo on the towel, stuck her middle finger into the jar, and in one motion bent down to take Ricardo's cock in her mouth and reached behind his balls with her lubed-up finger to find his asshole. Her mouth gripped Ricardo's cock firmly, up and down, and her finger rotated around his asshole and then began to penetrate about half an inch into his ass.

Ricardo moaned. She lifted her head up, took her middle finger and dipped it into the jar again, getting a large dollop of lubricant onto the tip of her finger, looked at Ricardo and announced, "I'm going to fuck you, don Ricardo. I'm going to fuck you so hard." Then she reached down under his balls again, finding his asshole and working more lubrication up into his ass.

Then she returned to his cock, holding it firmly by the shaft while sucking the top. Then she took the dildo and began to twist it, slowly, back and forth into his ass. She worked it in and out, twisting left and right, pushing it deeper. The muscles of his rectum refused to relax at first. She lifted her head up towards his head and whispered, "Let me fuck you. Let me in," and then returned to sucking his cock. At one point she stopped, pulled the dildo almost all the way out, added more lubricant with her finger to the dildo, and reinserted it up his ass. Finally came that moment when his rectum seemed to just relax all at once and invite the dildo all the way in. Alma sensed it and began to fuck him rhythmically with the dildo while she sucked him.

Ricardo was in some ecstatic heaven—he had no idea where. The feel of the dildo going in and out of his ass was exciting in some ghastly way—it was the sensation of submitting, of surrendering, of being taken, of being fucked.

Now that the dildo was all the way inside him, Alma jumped up, and went to the bathroom. Ricardo heard her washing her hands. Then she returned to the bed and reached up to the base of the dildo. There must have been a switch, because suddenly the dildo began to hum and vibrate fast. Alma took his cock back into her mouth and began to suck hard. She used one hand to squeeze his shaft and the other hand to twist his balls hard. She was so good—the squeezing and twisting were just this side of pain. He could feel how hard his erection was.

Then she straightened up, reached over to the top drawer one last time, and took out a leather strap with metal snaps on it. She wrapped the cock strap around his cock and balls, pulling it tight and snapping the metal fasteners together to form a tight cock ring. Then, just sitting there, she reached up, grabbed the dildo at the base, moved it in and out of him as it was vibrating, laughed and said, "I am fucking you don Ricardo, fucking you in your ass." She laughed again, and pushed the dildo back in, then climbed over his cock and lowered herself down, so now he was fucking her. Her pussy was tight and warm. She began to go up and down slowly, using her thigh muscles to raise and lower herself, placing her hands on his stomach for support. On the downstroke, she ground her pelvis into his, so his cock was as deep inside her as it could go. Ricardo's head was back, his eyes clenched shut, his mouth open, as she rode him, increasing the speed up and down, up and down, while the dildo vibrated in his ass. Then she reached forward with both hands, grabbed his two nipples between her thumbs and forefingers and twisted them while riding him even faster.

He wanted to make some kind of noise but all that came out of his throat was a faint "oh God, oh God, oh God," as he started to come. Alma clenched her vaginal walls so tight that he could feel his cum traveling up his cock and shooting out... one... two... three... pulsating spurts.

She ground her pelvis down on his cock one last time, wiggled it back and forth as if to shake his cock inside her, and then climbed off of him. Every muscle in his body seemed to have just stopped working. She reached up between his legs, switched off the dildo, and eased it out of him with one hand, and then used the other hand to unsnap the cock strap. She took both the dildo and cock strap into the bathroom room and returned with a clean towel, draped the towel over his pelvis, rolled him over, and moved some lever on the handcuffs to release them. Then she rolled him onto his back, patted his shoulder fondly, and stood up. Other than moving his arms out from under his back and stretching his wrists for a moment, Ricardo could not move. He just lay there, half staring at the ceiling, half looking at her.

"I'm going to go wash up," she said, "You take as much time as you need to get dressed." And she walked out of the room, closing the door behind her.

Ricardo lay there for several minutes. Finally, one thought came into his head, and he said it out loud. *Fuck, that was good.*

A few minutes later, he managed to get up, and make his way over to the shower.

*   *   *

He had no sense of how much time had passed. After he managed to shower and clean himself, and after slowly getting dressed, he checked his watch. Almost two hours exactly. She was a pro.

He made his way downstairs using the banister rail for support. Jenny was sitting there. Alma, of course, was nowhere in sight.

"Feeling better?" Jenny asked.

"Yes, Jenny, thank you. She's very, very good."

"Good," Jenny said, "would you like some tea?"

"No, no thank you, but could you do me a favor and call a cab. I don't think I can manage taking the bus home tonight."

Jenny laughed and got up to go to the phone, saying, "Well, that's proof enough for me."

*   *   *

The cab fare from La Chorrera to Villa Rosario was fifteen dollars, versus the bus fare of about a dollar, but tonight Ricardo was willing to pay. He didn't want to walk or wait. He felt barely able to function.

He forgot all about dinner. Once he got back to his apartment in Villa Rosario, he just stripped down and climbed into bed. No dinner. No drinking. Just a deep, deep, dreamless sleep.

Chapter 9:   The Texting Life

For the next two days, life seemed to return to normal. It was true that there were no emails from Carolina, nor any replies from Marco. But there were also no bad dreams. Life took on the timeless limbo existence that Ricardo loved about Panama: sunny days, cool nights, sitting at his desk writing during the day and sitting on his patio drinking Sangría and watching the sunset in the evening.

Everyone has their own level, their particular plateau—whether it be longitude, latitude, or moral level—in which they feel the most comfort, the most homeostatic with the world. For Ricardo, his level, his paradise, was living in Villa Rosario. Here, he could write undisturbed, and have his little trysts in La Chorrera whenever the need struck him.

He had put aside working on the *Old Man and the Semen* for the time being. It made him think of the brujo and he didn't like that. But the short stories were coming one after the other, so he was happy. He had finished the story about Heath the rock-climber the day before and had mailed it off to his publisher. On this particular morning, he was working hard on a short story about a young man named Thomas who is blinded in a car accident. Thomas is not bad-looking, and despite his blindness, makes a good living working at a call center where he talks to customers all day. In due time he meets a woman named Helen and they begin to date. Helen is a woman of great heart and kindness who actually loves Thomas, but Thomas becomes obsessed about whether Helen is "beautiful enough" for him—so obsessed that he eventually destroys the relationship.

Ricardo was intrigued with the idea of a man who was flawed, not just metaphorically blind but actually blind, yet who demanded perfect beauty in his partner. He thought it was representative of how most people lived their lives.

On this particular day he had, as usual, spent most of the morning writing, taking a break around one o'clock for a bite of lunch on his patio. Sometimes, depending on what he ate for lunch and on how hot the day was, he would take a nap in the afternoon, but on this particular afternoon, he was not sleepy. He was eager to return to his writing. He took his plate and glass back inside his apartment and washed them, then refilled his coffee mug, and went back to his computer.

He discovered that he had received two emails while he had been out on his patio. One was from his publisher, commenting positively on the story about Cindy and updating him on book sales. But the second was from Carolina. He opened it and read:

"Sorry I've out of touch recently. Leslie and I are in counseling together. We've decided to try and make this relationship work. We're going to a couples' retreat over spring break, so I won't be able to come down and see you. Sorry. Miss you much and so wanted to visit. You mean the world to me. Maybe this summer."

Ricardo sat back, and said out loud, *Well, that settles that*. He read her email again, thought for a moment, read it a third time, and then typed a reply: "Good for you. Stay in touch." No point in saying anything more, he thought. Then he went back out to his patio chair and sat down to think.

So, she wasn't coming to visit... okay. Obviously this relationship with Leslie was front and center. That was okay with him too. But he didn't like that she hadn't shared it with him until it had blown up. And he didn't understand how much of her panic about the university investigation might have really been about Leslie. But, evidently, it wasn't going to be his problem anymore. He thought about how long he had known Carolina, and the fun times they had had in Hamburg before he left for Panama. There was a time when they had been very close, but then he left, and then the correspondence dwindled while she was busy getting her doctorate. And while he always made it a point to see her when he traveled back to the States, their visits had gotten shorter over the past few years. His overriding conclusion was simple and unavoidable: He just didn't know her anymore. He had all these visual memories of her—her face, her laugh, the way she talked and moved... but they were all mental images from the past. And the past was past. She had moved on with her life, and he wasn't going to be a part of it anymore, at least not in the way he had hoped. Oh well, he thought to himself. Oh well. He had been foolish to think he could recapture the past. Doubly foolish because they had never been lovers. And here he had spent a week thinking he could go back to being something they had never been. He remembered something he once wrote in a short story years earlier. *Most people are defective, but when it comes to relationships, men are true idiots.* Very true, he thought. But okay. Better to know now rather than have her come all the way to Panama to find out she was a stranger to him.

He did care about her, and in his own way, he did feel love for her, but he wondered to himself how it was possible. Who is it he loved? The Carolina he used to know? His memory of her? The possibility that might have existed at one time? He knew there was no answer. Love simply never made any sense. It seemed to exist despite the fact that he had no idea who the other person was on the receiving end. He thought of Pandora, releasing the evils of the world. Maybe that's all love is, he thought, just another form of hope.

But in any case, he thought, it's settled. He didn't have to understand it. It was settled. He could move on.

He got up, went back inside to his writing desk and began work again on his short story about Thomas and Helen. He got some good writing done for the next several hours.

By late afternoon, he felt finished for the day. He never liked to push too hard after a good spell of writing. No point in pissing off the muses. He was about to close his laptop when he got another email. It was from Miguel, his friend in La Chorrera, asking if Ricardo wanted to meet him at the bathhouse tomorrow afternoon. Why not? Ricardo thought. He hadn't heard from Marco, and he wasn't quite ready to go see Alma again, so he typed back a reply to Miguel: "Yes, that would be nice. 1:00 good for you?" And Miguel, with his usual efficiency, replied immediately: "Yes, amigo, see you then."

Good, Ricardo thought. *Something to look forward to.*

Chapter 10:   The Bathhouse

The next afternoon, Ricardo took the bus to La Chorrera and met Miguel at the bathhouse. Ricardo knew not to be late. Miguel was the only Panamanian he ever met who was a stickler about time. Ricardo often teased him by saying, "You're more German than Panamanian." But Ricardo understood why. Miguel was the co-owner and manager of Los Cuñados, a popular restaurant in La Chorrera. Running a successful restaurant required efficiency and timeliness.

Ricardo met Miguel years ago, when Ricardo was first exploring Panama as a retirement option. They had met in that same bathhouse in La Chorrera and became lovers. After a year or so, they stopped being lovers but remained close friends. They often went to the bathhouse as cruising buddies, usually twice a month. In fact, Miguel had been his friend longer than anyone else in Panama, and Ricardo took great comfort in that.

Ricardo arrived at the bathhouse exactly at one o'clock, paid his entrance fee, and stepped inside to receive his towel, sandals, and locker key. Miguel was waiting for him in the locker room as usual. They greeted each other, stripped down, and went off to shower and then to sit in the hot tub. Over the years, their visits to the bathhouse together had taken on a certain rhythm, a certain ritual. They would always go first to the hot tub and sit and soak for twenty or thirty minutes and just talk. Even though they were naked, and the wall tiles around the hot tub contained illustrations of men having sex, there was nothing sexual about their time in the hot tub—it was simply two old friends getting together to talk, no different than two old men who might meet every morning at a certain park bench to chat and feed the pigeons.

The hot tub was large enough to hold about ten men, but Miguel and Ricardo almost always had the entire tub to themselves, as all the other men in the bathhouse were in the dark steam room, cruising for sex within its twisting corridors and obscured corners. Eventually Miguel and Ricardo would venture there as well. But first they always sat in the wonderfully bubbling water of the hot tub and caught up on the events in each other's lives. There was a large skylight over the hot tub which filled the room with light—which is why Ricardo always assumed that the other patrons never spent much time in the hot tub room... because the search for anonymous sex requires darker spaces.

Ricardo knew Miguel well enough to always start off their get-togethers by inquiring into how the restaurant business was going. Running a restaurant was a headache—there was always something to complain about—and the sooner that Miguel could get that day's complaints off his chest, the sooner they could move on to discussing other topics. As so it was today:

"We had a table of gringos in last night, from the state of Georgia I think they said," Miguel was explaining to Ricardo. "I love your people, Ricardo. Hell, my business depends on them. But explain to me why they are always so loud. Gringos are loud about everything! They talk loud; they laugh loud; they yell loud; they even drink loud. Why is this? Whenever a gringo party of four or more makes a reservation, I always put them in a separate room, away from any Panameño table, behind a wall or behind plants... anything to keep their noise down."

Ricardo laughed, and then joked, "It's because they can't hear, Miguel. Their ears are too small. Have you ever looked at their ears? Tiny little earholes. God cursed gringos by giving them little earholes, so they can't hear well. That's why they are so loud. They want to be sure the other gringos can hear them. And that's why they always have to ask your waiters to repeat themselves. It's not because your waiters don't speak English well. It's because the gringos can't hear them. Tiny little earholes."

Miguel laughed. "That's funny, my friend. I will have to tell my waiters that. I will have to tell them with a straight face so they believe me. Because they get mad when the gringos can't understand them. Maybe if they think it's a deformity, they won't get mad."

"Well, it is a deformity of a sort," Ricardo said. "Definitely a handicap. I must admit, I don't understand it myself. But it's true. Not just here, but all over the world. You go to any country and sit in a restaurant. You can always pick out the *norteamericanos*, because they will be the loudest group. To me, it's embarrassing."

"You are different, my friend. You are quiet."

"Yes, well... anyway, did the gringos tip well?"

"Of course! That's why the waiters all like to work the gringo tables—they do tip. Unlike Panamanians, who know that the tip is included in the bill, gringos always think they have to tip off the bill total. Makes the waiters happy."

"Did Marco wait on them?" Ricardo asked.

"Oh no, don Ricardo, I thought you knew. Marco quit last week."

"What? Really? Shit, no, I didn't know that."

"He did not tell you?" Miguel asked.

"Well, no, I haven't talked to him since we got back from Hotel de Sevilla. We talked about getting together for lunch, but he told me he had to work the next six days straight, and I haven't heard from him since. I assumed he was working."

"He worked for three days after he got back," explained Miguel, "but then he quit."

"Did he get another job somewhere?" Ricardo asked.

"I don't know. I never ask. Waiters come and go. It's a constant problem in the restaurant business. But I can tell you this: he won't find a better wait job than my restaurant. The hours are long, but I treat people right."

"I know you do, Miguel, I know you do," Ricardo said softly.

Ricardo looked down. The feeling of being left out,

that he had felt when he had seen Marco's Facebook pictures at the beach, returned to him. He just didn't understand. They had been so close in Hotel de Sevilla, had talked about their lives, their interests... they had kissed and laughed and slept together. Marco had even told him how much he liked working at Los Cuñados. How could Marco not tell him he was quitting? It just made no sense.

"Ah, mi amigo," Miguel suddenly said, "I can see you cared for him more than I thought. I am sorry. It was thoughtless of me to bring it up."

Ricardo took a deep breath, and said, "No, no, Miguel, you're fine. I just didn't know. Like I said, I haven't seen him since we got back. I sent him an email the other day asking if he wanted to have lunch, but he didn't respond to that either. I hope everything's okay with him."

Miguel looked at Ricardo and then said, "Well, my friend, he seemed fine when he quit. If he had family problems or something, I would have been able to tell, but he was not distressed. I am sorry. You two had a good time at Hotel de Sevilla?"

"Yeah, yeah, we did. I kind of liked him, Miguel. I guess I was hoping for, I don't know, for a continuing relationship."

"I see, I see." Miguel reached over and touched Ricardo's arm, lowered his voice and said, "You know, my friend, he is young, I think twenty-five, and you and I, well let's face it, we are not young. You cannot let yourself have feelings for these *muchachos*. They are more fickle than women. It is okay to fuck them. It is okay to love spending time with them. But you cannot let yourself love them. They are too young to understand love. They think love is a feeling. So when they become enchanted by someone else or some other feeling, they flitter off like butterflies... beautiful butterflies."

Ricardo just nodded his head. Miguel continued, "Trust me, amigo, I know. I want you to learn from my mistakes. We are old men now. We can still have great sex. We can still enjoy the young men. But love... love is different for old men. It is... how to say... out of our reach. Love can only be between equals. And these beautiful young men, they are not equals... they are not *our* equals. If you expect a relationship with them, you will be hurt. Pursue them, use them, enjoy them... but do not care for them."

Ricardo just continued to nod his head. He didn't like hearing Miguel say that all he could hope for was to use young men for sex. It seemed harsh. But at a certain level, he knew Miguel was right.

Miguel continued to talk gently to Ricardo. "This is why I love this bathhouse, don Ricardo. It is perfect for men like you and me. Once you step into the steam room, no relationships are possible. It's such a paradox, no? In the dark, we are no longer old men, but in the dark, no relationships are possible. There is all the love you want, but no relationships. And afterwards, you can wash your sins away and you leave here feeling clean and unencumbered by the vicissitudes of age or the failures of other people. The steam room is a beautiful place, don Ricardo. Come on, let's go into the steam room, and we will let the heat and the steam melt away your expectations of a relationship with that boy. Come on, don Ricardo. Life is a buffet table and the world is full of pretty young waiters."

Ricardo laughed at Miguel's silly metaphor, but he stood up, and both he and Miguel made their way into the steam room.

Ricardo had to agree with Miguel on one thing: he did think that this bathhouse in La Chorrera had the most perfect steam room of any gay bathhouse he had ever been to. There was a large square main room, steamy and lit by soft blue lights. The steam took on the blue color of the lights. It was ethereal. There you could dimly see who you were fondling or who was blowing you. And the only sound was the soft hissing of the steam, or the wet slurping of someone sucking someone in the corner. With a regular frequency, the hissing was interrupted by the moans of someone cumming.

Several different corridors ran off the sides of the steam room. There was steam in these corridors, but no light—it was pitch black. One corridor led to a maze, a steamy labyrinth of completely dark twists and turns. These were places where the shy, the old, and the ugly could slowly feel their way along the steamy wall, totally blind in the blackness, for the sole purpose of bumping into another blind wanderer, which of course led to feeling each other's bodies, especially the cocks. It was a great place to spend thirty or forty minutes fondling a multitude of cocks. But there were no places to sit in this corridor. Blow jobs thus required either awkwardly bending over or getting down on one's knees on the hard, concrete floor, so mostly the men just used their hands, feeling each other while embracing. The other corridor was not a maze but had several small rooms off to each side, where there were concrete benches built into the wall where one could sit or lean. This corridor, equally black and blind, was for men who preferred to sit while blowing a stranger. The concrete benches also provided a place to lean for someone getting fucked from behind.

Ricardo liked the maze corridor. It was a great place to get worked up safely. Fondling and hand jobs were always safe, and Ricardo never gave blowjobs in this or any other bathhouse. Years ago, he used to carry a small bag of condoms that he would attach to the wristband that held his locker key. Years ago, if he really wanted to blow someone in a bathhouse, he would quickly remove a condom from the bag, roll it on their cock, and blow them. He had learned to do this quickly and deftly, but still it required extra effort. So eventually, he simply gave it up and refused to give any oral sex in a bathhouse. And, of course... never any anal sex. One had to be responsible. One had had to be responsible for many years. He remembered, when he was a young man—before HIV exploded onto the world—when he was just discovering the bathhouses of Europe. What a liberation it was to blow and be blown, to fuck and be fucked, by *anyone* in the bathhouse who was attractive. He was a young man then, and thus many found him attractive as well, and the sex was endless. All afternoon, into the night, sometimes all night, finally sleeping cuddled in groups in large rooms with mattresses on the floor for just that purpose, and then crawling home in the dreary light of dawn as other people—fools, he thought back then—were making their way to work.

But that was decades ago, and he had lost many friends to AIDS, and thus he had adapted, and he had survived. So now, the bathhouses were all about stimulation, all about the quiet joy of watching young naked men prance by the hot tub where he and Miguel might be soaking, and simply enjoying watching their cocks, flaccid or semi-erect, bounce up and down as they walked by. Or wandering in the dark corridors, blindly feeling bodies, cocks, scrotums, hair, running his hand over stomachs and asses, reaching down and grabbing some new cock, always wondering what it would feel like—short and thick, or long and straight, or curved, circumcised or not—before moving on in the dark to feel another, and then another, and another. Or sitting in the steam room watching other naked men fucking and sucking each other. Stimulation was the name of the game now.

Ricardo and Miguel went into the steam room and took seats next to each other on the large concrete steps that served as seats. Both men removed their towels, indicating they were open to being touched. It was a busy day in the bathhouse and the steam room was active. Off to Ricardo's left, on the next level of steps going up, a young man had laid his towel out on the step and had lain face down on it, with his legs apart. Another man had climbed up behind him, hunched down, and had moved his legs even further apart and was starting to kiss and lick his ass, moving deeper and deeper between the cheeks, to lick the man's asshole. The prone man was responding by arching his butt into the other face. Off to Ricardo's right, just past Miguel, another man had sat down. This man had no body hair whatsoever—he had shaved it completely off, making his large cock appear even larger. He did, however, have gold nipple rings, along with a ring though the end of his cock. He was stroking himself, angling his cock toward anyone who walked by. Soon another man took the invitation, got down on his knees and began to suck the hairless man.

Other men walked by, letting their hands traipse across either or both of Ricardo's and Miguel's thighs, and occasionally pausing to fondle either or both cocks. Both

Ricardo and Miguel were getting hard now.

Then a young darker Panamanian lad walked by, slim with hardly any hips. He was cute, Ricardo thought. The young man paused in front of Ricardo, smiled shyly, and then moved off to a corner. Ricardo got up and followed him. The lad had sat down on the first large concrete step. Ricardo sat down next to him, smiled, and reached over to his cock. It was not large, but long and uncircumcised. Ricardo began to stroke it. The young man's cock sprang to attention almost immediately upon being touched. *This boy's horny,* Ricardo thought as he tightened his grip. The young man then shifted his position and moved to sit astride Ricardo, facing him, so that Ricardo's erect cock was now standing next to the lad's cock. Ricardo wrapped his hand around both cocks at once and began a steady up-down stroke. The lad first rubbed Ricardo's chest, then eased himself forward until he was lying on top of Ricardo and began kissing Ricardo's upper chest and neck. *Clearly, a fellow starved for attention,* Ricardo thought. The boy was short and slim, but even so, the weight of him on Ricardo made it difficult for Ricardo to keep masturbating the two cocks—his hand being blocked by the lad's stomach on the upstroke. But he continued, because he liked the feeling of the young man wanting him.

On the steps above where Ricardo was sitting, several other men were sitting, both to the upper left and right of Ricardo. Ricardo was aware of them when he first sat down but had not looked at them because he was focused on the young man. But now he was aware of the man to his upper left inching his way towards Ricardo. There were three levels of steps in this part of the steam room, and the size and design of the steps was such that the second level, where this man was sitting, was at a height that allowed the man's knees to be the same level as Ricardo's head. Ricardo was not interested in letting anyone else join him and the lad, so he turned to look at the man sitting above him in order to shake his head no. The steam was much denser up at the second level, but Ricardo could see that this was an older man, short and stocky, with white hair and a white mustache. Ricardo stopped stroking the lad and squinted to make out the man's features, but he couldn't see his face well in the steam. But he could see that the old man had a large dark cock surrounded by thick hair—and the old man was holding it and aiming it toward Ricardo. It was semi-erect, and the foreskin was half-pulled back from the head. The way that the blue lights glowed on the old man's cock and balls seemed to illuminate them in a soft blue light. All at once it seemed to Ricardo that he could see electric blue semen pulsating inside the man's scrotum, and he knew that the old man wanted Ricardo to suck his cock. Ricardo began to panic. He shook his head no, but the old man just inched closer. The weight of the lad on Ricardo's torso and chest was holding him down—he couldn't move. He pulled his right hand out from under the lad, and placed both hands on the young man's shoulder's and tried to push him off, but the lad just lay there. Ricardo realized that the lad had both of his arms wrapped around Ricardo and was not letting go. He turned and looked again at the old man. The steam had cleared a bit, and Ricardo could see it was definitely the brujo. He was sitting right next to Ricardo now. Ricardo pushed the lad on his chest harder, and started to hit the lad's shoulders. The brujo swung his right leg over Ricardo's head, so he was sitting right over Ricardo. The brujo's cock was now pressing against Ricardo's cheek. Ricardo could feel it hot and erect. The brujo moved it with his hand so the head brushed against Ricardo's mouth. Ricardo turned his head away, raised his right hand and struck the lad hard on the side of the lad's head. The lad cried out, and jerked up, looking at Ricardo in alarm, and leaped off him. At the same time, Ricardo ducked his head past the brujo's cock and pushed himself off the concrete step with both hands, but lost his footing on the wet floor, and fell. He banged his head against the opposite wall and saw stars.

He could hear the sound of bare feet scurrying in the steam. Miguel ran up, kneeled down, and helped Ricardo to his feet.

"What happened, don Ricardo? Did you fall?" Miguel asked.

"Get me out of here," was all Ricardo could say.

Miguel helped Ricardo up and half-carried him out of the steam room. Ricardo was touching the side of his head carefully, to see if he could feel any blood. Miguel walked him to one of the well-lit shower stalls near the hot tub, turned the shower water to cool, and guided Ricardo under it, so that the cool water gently flowed over Ricardo's head.

"It was very hot in there today, my friend," Miguel was saying. "I think you must have fainted. Here, let me look at your head."

Miguel examined the side of Ricardo's head. "No blood, but you will have a knot there for sure. Come on, let's go sit down."

"I didn't faint, Miguel," Ricardo said.

"Let's go sit down," Miguel repeated, and took Ricardo by the arm and led him into a small room with tables next to the hot tub area. This was the area where men could sit and relax. There was a bar along one wall that sold soft drinks and snacks. Miguel sat Ricardo down at one of the tables and went over to the bar and got two cokes with ice and brought them back to the table.

"Here, drink this. The sugar will help."

"I didn't faint," Ricardo repeated.

"Fainting, falling, it makes no difference, don Ricardo. You still hit your head," Miguel replied. "Sit and drink your coke."

"Someone was trying to make me suck them..." Ricardo started to say, but Miguel just raised his hand gently and said, "Just relax for a minute, don Ricardo. Drink your coke. I want to see if you are going to be alright, or whether we should go to the hospital."

Ricardo stopped talking and took a sip of his coke. It was very sweet but tasted good. His head did throb badly where he had banged it. It hurt so bad that it almost made him want to cry, but he tried to pull himself together. He looked around the room. The other tables were empty. The fellow behind the bar was cleaning some glasses. There was a TV on the wall showing gay porn without any sound, just the image of a large dick penetrating someone's asshole. Ricardo looked at these things to see how his vision was. He seemed able to focus his eyes okay. He moved his head left and right; his neck seemed fine. There was just the throbbing pain on the side of his forehead. But the pain was slightly less now. He did not think he had hit that hard, at least not hard enough to do any damage.

He looked at Miguel. Miguel was staring into Ricardo's eyes, first the left eye and then the right eye, back and forth. Ricardo knew what Miguel was doing—he was looking for any difference in pupil size, to ascertain whether Ricardo had suffered a concussion.

"I'm fine, Miguel," he said. "I'm feeling better now."

"Good, my friend. But let's just sit for a while."

Ricardo looked around the room again. Then he decided not to tell Miguel that the man who accosted him was a brujo. Now was not the right time. Miguel would just misconstrue it as a proof of a concussion, as some mental confusion. He would tell him at some point, but not today. But he did ask him, "Miguel, did you see that older man, up on the second tier? He had white hair and a white mustache? Sitting right above where I was sitting?"

"No, don Ricardo, I did not notice him. Why?"

"Oh, he was the one who tried to make me suck him. There was a young boy lying on my chest, and I couldn't move, and that old man was going to stick his dick in my mouth."

"Ha," laughed Miguel, "you are very popular, don Ricardo."

"No. No, it wasn't good. I didn't want to do it. But I couldn't move because that boy was lying on me. I had to hit him to get him off me."

"You hit him?" asked Miguel.

"Yeah, I slapped him pretty damn hard. You didn't hear him yell?"

"I heard something, some kind of commotion, but when I looked up, all I could see was you lying on the floor. There was no one else around."

"Really? You didn't see that old man at all? Short, stocky man, very dark, white hair and white mustache?

"No señor. I did not see anyone like that."

"How about the boy? Cute, young, very slim?"

"No, no. I just saw you get up and walk over to the corner. Then a minute or two later, I heard a noise and you were on the floor."

"Hmmm... okay, okay," said Ricardo, and took another sip of coke. "Can we get out of here?"

"In a minute, don Ricardo. First sit and relax, then we can go. I will call a cab and take you to my restaurant and make you some lunch. Maybe put some ice on your head." Miguel reached up and gently touched Ricardo's head at his jaw line to move his head to the side. Miguel looked at the side of Ricardo's head. "Yes, I think some ice will be good."

Chapter 11:   Ice

By the time Miguel and Ricardo had gotten dressed and caught a taxi over to Los Cuñados, the pain in Ricardo's head had settled down to a dull ache. Nonetheless, Miguel filled a small bag with ice, and had Ricardo hold it to his head while Miguel made a sandwich for him. Ricardo sat on a wooden barstool in the kitchen watching Miguel deftly slice bread and tomatoes while grilling a piece of chicken for the sandwich. The restaurant didn't open until four for dinner, so no one else was there yet. Ricardo looked around. The kitchen was well organized, with a large butcher block counter in the center of the room for cutting and preparing food, surrounded by three stove tops with a built-in gas grill, two ovens, two refrigerators, and a massive freezer. Twenty or more cutting knives were stuck to magnetic strips on the wall, and pots and pans hung from metal hooks from the wooden beams overhead. On each worktable there was also a wooden block that held different types of kitchen knives.

"I am making you a sandwich," Miguel said.

"I see that," Ricardo replied.

"No, I mean, we don't eat these here. I just keep the ingredients in case some gringo asks for one. I think you call this 'comfort food'. Ha. I think they are confusing. Too much bread. But I make it for you. You had a nasty fall."

"Eh, I'm feeling a bit better now. I think I'll be okay."

"Just keep that ice on your head. It'll help. It'll take a while for this chicken to cook."

"I appreciate it, Miguel."

While Miguel was tending to the food, Ricardo

thought back to the bathhouse. Miguel hadn't seen either the slim boy or the brujo; hadn't noticed the slim boy come up to Ricardo while Ricardo was sitting next to Miguel; hadn't noticed that Ricardo had followed the lad over to the corner; hadn't seen the brujo sitting above Ricardo; hadn't seen any sex between Ricardo and anyone in the corner; hadn't seen the slim boy enveloping Ricardo; hadn't noticed the brujo moving so as to straddle Ricardo's head; hadn't noticed any struggle; didn't hear the boy cry out when Ricardo hit him; and didn't see anyone scramble away into the dark stream after Ricardo hit the floor. Miguel had said that he had only seen Ricardo get up from where they were sitting together in the steam room and wander off alone. He hadn't noticed anything else until he "heard a commotion" and saw Ricardo on the ground. Okay, Ricardo thought, okay, it's possible that Miguel didn't see any of it. After all, Ricardo couldn't remember noticing any of the men that Miguel might have been playing with, either. And it was dark and steamy. But Ricardo rejected the idea that it didn't happen. He didn't make it up. He didn't walk over to the corner, slip, hit his head, and then reconstruct some hallucination as he was coming to, because of the blow to his head. There was no dreamlike quality to what had happened. The events had happened in a total real-time sequence. Ricardo knew this in his bones. It had happened. But this presented a real problem. Who was the old man with the white hair and the white mustache? Ricardo ran through the logical sequence: either it was the brujo or just an old man. If it was a just some old man, well, he had behaved in a way that was much too aggressive for bathhouse behavior. Men just don't force themselves on other men in the bathhouse, especially when one of them clearly indicates no. Plus, it seemed to Ricardo that there was an odd coordination between the young lad and the old man. The young lad had led him over to that particular corner. And once there, the boy sat on Ricardo and wrapped his arms around him in such a way that Ricardo could not move away from the old man. Even when Ricardo started to push on the boy's shoulders, the lad didn't seem to notice. Again, very unusual for bathhouse etiquette. But logically, it could have been either a massive coincidence, a perfect storm of two newcomers to the bathhouse—a lonely boy and an aggressive old man—who both thought that it would be okay to ignore all the normal signals in bathhouse culture. The only other possibility was that the old man *was* the brujo, and was either taking advantage of the situation with the young boy wrapped around Ricardo, or was in cahoots with the young boy, to trap Ricardo in the corner, to force him to suck his cock, to force him to swallow the blue semen. But that thought just made Ricardo's head hurt more. To believe that would mean that the brujo was real, that he was stalking Ricardo, first in his dreams, then in real life. And that was just too implausible to accept. Fear is something so primal in our evolutionary history, so instinctual, so necessary for our survival that Ricardo had to fight to gain mental control over believing that someone could be so psychic as to step into his dreams and then step into his actual life. It was believable only if he gave in to fear. But it simply wasn't logical. And while he absolutely believed that what he *saw* was real—an old man pushing for a blowjob—he knew that the meaning that the mind *ascribes* to things is something else. The mind is fear-based. Evolution has ensured that. And the meaning that his mind wanted to overlay onto what actually happened was some primal supernatural story, only believable on a level of fear and raw emotion.

And thus Ricardo, moment by moment, gained control over his panic. As he did so, the pain in his head abated, things became more in-focus, and he felt better.

"Here's your sandwich, señor." Miguel's announcement brought Ricardo out of his logic trance.

"Oh, thank you, Miguel. It smells wonderful. Aren't you eating?" Ricardo asked.

"No, I will eat with my staff when they arrive in an about thirty minutes."

"Okay, I'll clear out by then," Ricardo said, as he took a bite of the sandwich.

"No hurry, mi amigo. You cannot leave until I think you are well enough."

Ricardo smiled. The sandwich was excellent. He was feeling much better. Miguel was a good friend.

*   *   *

On the bus ride back to Villa Rosario, Ricardo thought long and hard again about the brujo. He realized that he did not have to decide one way or the other about him. It was not a question of whether it was an aggressive old man, or a magical brujo in the bathhouse. It could be either one. Ricardo decided that he could simply hold both options open until he had more data.

The pain in his head had reduced to the point of just being a headache, although the area where he had hit was still tender to the touch. But he decided that he had not hit his head very hard. He also resolved to be more careful about his movements in the future. He was older now and couldn't afford to fall too many times.

As usual, the bus let him off in front of the Parque Central in Villa Rosario, right in front of the Catholic Church. He looked up at the Church, at its ancient dull white walls and towers, the many steps upward to the massive wooden doors. Off to one side, almost unnoticeable, stood the tiny house where Father Lopez lived. Ricardo just stood there looking, his eyes going back and forth from the steeple and the bell tower to the tiny house in the back, and back to the bell tower. He hadn't planned on this, but he found himself walking up through the iron gate in front of the church, up the steps, then to the side around the Church, following an old stone walkway, through a small garden, to the door of the tiny house, and then, without thinking, as if some force was moving his hand, he knocked upon the door.

Chapter 12:   Father Lopez

There was no answer to Ricardo's knock. He waited a few minutes, and then knocked again, this time louder, in case the old cleric was hard of hearing. Still no answer. Ricardo felt both disappointed and a bit relieved. Although he wanted to talk with Father Lopez, Ricardo still didn't know what he was going to say to him.

But as he turned to walk away, he looked and saw that coming slowly up the stone walkway, was an old priest with a cane. He recognized him, because someone had pointed him out to Ricardo a year or two ago, one time when the old priest was sitting in the park.

The old priest did not seem surprised to see someone at his door. Ricardo just stood there, as the old cleric made his way, leaning on the cane up to the house.

"Padre Lopez," Ricardo said in Spanish, "*Disculpe,* but I would like to talk with you."

"I don't do confessions anymore," the old cleric stated flatly and without looking at Ricardo, Father Lopez stepped around him to the front door of his cottage. "You need to see the priest in the Church for confession."

"I'm not here for confession, Padre," Ricardo blurted out. "I'm here to talk to you about the brujo."

Father Lopez stopped, turned around slowly, and looked at Ricardo. He looked him up and down, and then said, "You must be señor Ricardo."

Ricardo felt a wave of fear go through him. "How... how did you know?" he managed to say.

"Jenny told me about you," Father Lopez said matter-of-factly. "You should go to confession more... but alright, come on in."

The old cleric opened the door to his cottage and stepped inside. Ricardo followed him in.

The inside of the cottage was simple: a concrete floor, a wooden table with two chairs, a sink with a hotplate by a window, a squat antique refrigerator, and an old easy chair with a reading lamp in the corner. Books were piled on the floor in front of a small bookshelf that was full of more books.

The old cleric turned on a light switch on the wall. A small bare electric bulb over the table lit up. "Sit down," Father Lopez said, pointing to one of the chairs at the table. Ricardo sat down.

Father Lopez shuffled over to the kitchenette and pulled a small juice jar from the sink, looked at it in the light of the window, rinsed it out, and placed it on the counter. Then he got another glass from a side cupboard, and then a bottle from below the sink. He brought both glasses and the bottle over to the table and sat down. He looked at Ricardo's face, his eyes, and then at the side of Ricardo's head where a small reddish knot had formed.

"Ah, I see you have met the brujo," Father Lopez announced. "*That* is why you are here."

Ricardo didn't know what to say. He realized his mouth was open and shut it. He just watched the old priest open the bottle, which Ricardo now realized was a wine bottle, and fill both glasses with wine. He pushed one glass towards Ricardo.

Ricardo wasn't sure what the formalities were; he had never sat and drank with a priest before. Would there be grace? Or a toast? But then he saw Father Lopez simply start to drink, so Ricardo did the same. He took a sip of the wine. It was harsh but drinkable. He took another sip and then said, "Padre Lopez, I don't know exactly where to start..."

"No need," Father Lopez interrupted. "I've seen it many times before. I will tell you what happened. You started having dreams about an old man staring at you. At first they were brief, and you didn't think anything of them. But they recurred, and for some reason, they interested you. And so you invited them back. There was something in the dreams you wanted. And they came back. At first it was okay, but then they started getting stronger. At some point, the old man in the dream became sexual... no, that's not right... he began to *mean something* sexual to you. And even though you were worried, you didn't tell him to go away. You wanted to know more, like Adam in the Garden. So, he came back even stronger. But at some point, you figured out he was a brujo. That was unusual. Most people don't figure that out. That was smart of you, because then you began to realize his power."

Father Lopez paused, as if he was searching for what to say next. "You were afraid. But you still did not reject him. So, he tested you. He came to you..." Father Lopez paused and looked again at the side of Ricardo's head. He reached up, took Ricardo's chin in his hand gently and turned Ricardo's head to the side and looked at the bump. "It looks like today. He came to you today and revealed himself directly to you. But you did not submit... not this time." Father Lopez released Ricardo's chin. His brow furrowed. "You got away, but it was not a fight. You ran. You only have one bruise..." He paused again, as if he was thinking of what to say. "It is unusual. Usually he takes young girls... sometimes young boys. But he prefers young girls... young girls who are a bit too sure of themselves; girls whose parents cannot control them. Girls whose parents are too backwards to ever tell them about their bodies. The brujo comes to them at night, to the ones at just the right age, and teaches them how to touch themselves. They think it is a miracle. He beguiles them, and they think they can trust him. Then eventually, when they are walking alone near a field or by a river, he appears to them, and introduces them to sex with a man. With the older girls or the boys, he is different, more intimidating. He overpowers them. But it's always sex with the brujo, never any other way... And usually with the young... sometimes the very young. So when Jenny told me about you, I did not know what to think. But then I looked around and I realized... we have no young girls of that exact age right now in our town. That's why so many people have been having dreams lately. The brujo is hunting. He's getting desperate. He is very hungry and he will take anyone... anyone who lets him. Anyone will do, even an old man like you. It *is* sex he is offering to you, correct?"

Ricardo was embarrassed to be so directly interrogated by a priest. He felt very exposed, but he nodded his head yes.

"Yes, it is always sex," Father Lopez continued. "I used to be judgmental. When some young boy came to me and told me about the brujo, I used to condemn the boy. That was a mistake. Sometimes the Church makes mistakes. We lost too many children. I wanted to tell the parents to teach their children about sex, but the Church forbade me..." The old cleric's voice trailed off. He reached for the bottle and refilled his glass, and then refilled Ricardo's glass. Ricardo had not even realized that he had drunk his glass empty, but he had.

"Padre... what will happen next? I mean, what will happen to me?" Ricardo asked.

"He may take you," Father Lopez answered matter-of-factly. "He is fairly powerful."

"Wait a minute," Ricardo protested. "What do you mean he may take me? I'm not going to let that happen."

"The only way to stop the brujo is to kill him. I have been telling don Fernando that for years, but don Fernando is conflicted. He says he does not want to take the law into his own hands, but I think he is afraid of the brujo. No, the only way to stop the brujo is to kill him and burn his body. But it is very difficult. No one sees him unless he comes to them."

"Don't you know where he lives?" Ricardo asked.

"Somewhere in the nearby hills."

"Well, where exactly?"

"No one knows. We burned his house here in Villa Rosario years ago, burned it to the ground... but everyone knows he escaped. We don't know how, but we searched through the ashes of the house and there were no bones. Since then, no one has seen him... except for the people who see him in dreams, or the people who invite him to appear in person."

"I did not invite him!" Ricardo almost shouted.

Father Lopez lifted his eyes and looked at Ricardo. He kept his eyes fixed on Ricardo and said simply and softly, "Yes, you did. The brujo only comes when invited."

Ricardo tried to contain his anger. He clamped down on his teeth, then he decided on a different tack. "How do you know he lives in the hills around here?"

"Because some of the young people have told us. Sometimes, in their dreams, they go with him to his house. They tell us it is a simple house in the hills, indistinguishable from any other house, but out of sight from the other houses around it... and that it backs against a hill. Over the years, all the children who have seen the house describe it the same way. They all claim they walk there from Villa Rosario in their dream. We have looked of course, but there are many, many hills around this town... and no one knows all the back roads of all the hills."

Ricardo was afraid to ask his next question, but he did anyway. "And what happened to all the children who saw his house?" he asked.

"Oh, they all disappeared, of course."

"Do you know of anyone who has escaped him?"

"Oh yes, there are several ways. Many people just leave town. That is the best solution. The brujo's power comes from his location here—he gets his power from the earth. So he cannot travel far, even in dreams. He can reach northeast to La Chorrera, northwest to Santa Rita, south to Lidice or Cermeno, but that's about it. You get beyond those towns, and you are safe. You can move to Panama City and you would be safe there."

"I don't want to move to Panama City," Ricardo replied.

"Or Santiago, or David, or back to the States... you can go anywhere."

"I don't want to leave. I like it here."

Father Lopez just shrugged his shoulders.

"Padre," Ricardo asked, "if I stay, how can I fight him?"

"Only by ceasing to invite him," came the terse reply.

Ricardo rolled his eyes. He wanted to shout out again that he wasn't inviting the brujo, but he knew that would be pointless. He thought for a second, then said, "Say more, Padre. How am I inviting him?"

"Something about the brujo interests you, makes you think about him. You want something from him. It may not be sex. Many of the young boys who have gone to him only wanted power or wealth and they thought that having sex with him was the only way to get that..."

"Wait a minute, Padre. What do you mean, having sex with him? Is that what he wants?" Ricardo asked.

"Isn't that obvious?" Father Lopez asked.

"Well... no... I mean, yes, he seems to want that, but then what?"

Father Lopez thought for a minute, then said, "I have counseled many young people who have had bad dreams. And I have talked to some young people to whom the brujo has appeared in person, and they have told me that he wants to have sex with them. Some of those people have escaped him by leaving town. But the rest simply disappeared. No one knows what happened to them. I only know that I have never talked with anyone who has had sex with him. To me, that means that once a person has sex with the brujo, he or she belongs to the brujo somehow. Maybe the sex kills them. Maybe he consumes their bodies. Maybe they are buried up in the hills. I do not know for a fact. All I know is that those people who were tempted, those who wanted something from the brujo, they all disappeared."

"And what is your personal belief about what happened to them?" Ricardo asked.

"My personal belief? Well, my personal belief is that the brujo is an anti-Christ... I think that once they take of his body, they become him, just as taking of the body and blood of Christ means that we become one with Christ."

Ricardo sat quietly for a minute. Father Lopez refilled both their wine glasses. Ricardo took another sip, and then said quietly, "You said the only way to stop him was to kill him. Can he be killed?"

"Of course. He may be a brujo, but he is just a man. But his body must be burned. It is not enough just to kill him. He must be burned completely."

"Why?" Ricardo asked.

Father Lopez looked surprised. "That is the tradition," he said. "The Church has always killed brujos by burning them, usually at the stake."

"Why?" Ricardo asked again.

Father Lopez smiled. It was the first time Ricardo had seen him smile. "I guess because it works," he said. "I don't have another answer." Father Lopez seemed to think for a bit then said, "That was our mistake fifteen years ago. We were following the old traditions. We thought it would be enough just to burn his house down, with him trapped inside. We should have caught him first, then burned his body. We had rifles. We had surrounded his house. We saw him go inside. We could have shot him. But we thought it would be enough to burn his house with him inside. But somehow he escaped. We should have shot him when we had the chance. He escaped and got smart. Now we do not know where he lives."

"And you think he is still here? Somewhere nearby?" Ricardo asked.

"Oh, I am sure of it. He cannot leave here. He is bound to this earth, to this place."

"Why do you say that, Padre?" Ricardo asked.

"Well, wherever a brujo is when he becomes a brujo, is where he must stay. He cannot leave. This place is what keeps him alive. As long as he can feed here, he will live here."

Something about the way Father Lopez said that last sentence reminded Ricardo of one of his early dreams about the old man and the magic semen, and Ricardo blurted out, "How old is this brujo, Padre?"

"We think 200 years, maybe older. We're not sure. Don Fernando's father once told me that *his* father knew him, and back then the brujo was middle-aged."

Chapter 13:   Manolito's

The more Ricardo listened to Father Lopez talk, the worse the pain in his head got, not from the bruise but from the information. The wine seemed to help some, and Ricardo decided he needed more. The evening was approaching. Ricardo said his goodbyes to Father Lopez, thanked him profusely, and then made his way back to his own apartment. On the way he stopped at the only *licorería* in town. He had plenty of Sangría at home, but he bought a bottle of guaro—a cheap sugarcane liquor—to mix with it. He didn't want to think anymore tonight. He just wanted to numb both his body and his mind.

He awoke the next morning about ten, much later than his usual rising hour. He opened his eyes and looked around. He was in his own bed. He didn't remember getting undressed and going to bed, but there were his clothes, thrown over his chair as usual, and he was clearly naked under the covers. His mouth was dry, and there was a dull ache in his head, but he knew it was from the drinking. The outside of his head felt better. He got up, went to the kitchen and drank two full glasses of lemonade from a pitcher he kept in the refrigerator. He found one banana left in a plastic box where he stored fruit, and he ate that. The liquid and the food helped. It wasn't a bad hangover, he decided. Probably ameliorated by having slept so long. At least he had not had any dreams about the brujo. In fact, he couldn't remember having any dreams at all.

One of the things that Father Lopez had told him the day before was that he probably wouldn't have any more brujo dreams. "Once the brujo appears in person," Father Lopez had said, "he no longer needs to use your dreams, unless you specifically invite him back to your dreams." Ricardo found that reassuring. He would much rather deal with an enemy in real life—in this world—than in the world of dreams. On that thought, he went over to the small desk of drawers where he kept his clothes and rummaged through the bottom drawer until he found a large pocketknife. It had a gravity-release mechanism which allowed it to slide open quickly. Ricardo had bought it in a dingy pawn shop years ago when he had first arrived in Panama City, when he was first exploring the country and wasn't sure what to expect. But he never had to use it, and the knife had sat in the bottom drawer for years. But now, Ricardo thought, he would re-deputize it and carry it with him, because one never knows.

After showering and getting dressed, Ricardo called Dan.

"Hey Dan, it's Ricardo. Do you want to catch some breakfast downtown, or maybe just coffee? I have some things I want to talk with you about."

Dan laughed. "It's a bit late for breakfast. Did you just get up?"

"Yeah."

"Well, I could do lunch in, say, forty-five minutes at Café Manolito."

"Yes," Ricardo replied. "Thanks, that would work fine. See you then."

Café Manolito was just a five-minute walk from his apartment, so Ricardo made a pot of coffee while he waited. While the coffee was brewing, he sat at his writing desk and made some notes on a 3x5 card of things he wanted to ask Dan. Had Dan talked to don Fernando? Did Dan know Father Lopez? If so, what did he think about him? What was Father Lopez's connection to don Fernando? And what the hell happened fifteen years ago with the fire at the brujo's house?

Making the notes brought back more of what Father Lopez had told him, and brought back the same worries he had experienced the night before. Father Lopez seemed to act as if Ricardo was doomed, as if his fate was sealed because the brujo had appeared to him. Ricardo just didn't believe that.

He also opened his laptop and checked his email. Nothing more from Carolina. He checked Marco's Facebook page. Marco had posted a picture of himself with friends at a restaurant the day before. Ricardo recognized the restaurant's name—it was in Panama City.

The rest of his emails were junk. He started to think that maybe he would send Marta an email that afternoon, but he quickly nixed that idea. He wasn't going to tell her about the brujo. And there wouldn't be much else to talk about. He closed his laptop. Then he remembered to take his blood pressure medicine.

*　*　*

Ricardo got to Café Manolito a few minutes before Dan. Manolito's didn't serve breakfast, so Ricardo ordered a *pollo casado*—chicken with rice and beans—and some fried plantain, along with *limonada hierbabuena*—lemonade with mint. Good hangover food, he thought. He sat down at one of the wooden tables to wait for Dan.

Like most of the food stands in Villa Rosario, Manolito's had a single counter where you ordered your food from the one employee who would then go into the back and cook it. There were just four small wooden tables on an open-air patio, shielded from the sun by an overhanging tin roof. It was too early for the usual lunch crowd, so Ricardo had the place to himself. Dan walked up a few minutes later. He waved at Ricardo, then walked up to the counter and yelled his food order at the man in the kitchen who was cooking Ricardo's lunch. The man nodded, and Dan came over and sat down across from Ricardo. The knot on the side of Ricardo's forehead had lessened, but the skin was still red. Ricardo saw Dan's eyes dart up to Ricardo's forehead and then back down.

"Late night?" Dan asked.

"Yeah."

"Jenny's?"

"No, just got into some guaro."

"Ouch. That stuff will hurt you," Dan said.

"Well, I don't drink it straight. But I like to pour it into my Sangría on occasion. Gives it a little kick."

"I bet it does. Is that how you bumped your head?" Dan asked, nodding his head toward Ricardo's bruise.

"Oh, yeah," Ricardo said. He wanted to talk to Dan about the brujo, but he wasn't going to talk about the bathhouse.

"So...what's up, dude?" Dan asked.

"Well, remember the last time I saw you? We got talking about that local brujo. Did you ever have a chance to talk with don Fernando about him?"

Dan frowned, looked directly at Ricardo, and said, "Yeah, I did. But let me ask you first, why the interest?"

Just like an ex-cop, Ricardo thought, but he said, "It's a long story, but I think I saw the guy."

"Really? Where?"

"In La Chorrera."

"Whereabouts in La Chorrera?"

"Doesn't matter. Just on some street. But I had the sense that he was, like, following me."

"How did you know it was him?" Dan asked.

"Well, I didn't!" Ricardo said in a slightly exasperating tone. "That's why I was wanting to know more."

"Okay," said Dan.

Ricardo could see Dan's eyes flitting left and right as he was thinking of how to respond. Finally Dan said, "Look, don Fernando's a friend. You're a friend too, but I've known don Fernando a long time. We have a certain... a certain business relationship. So I can't tell you all that he told me. But yes, I did talk with him, but I just can't talk much about what he told me about the brujo."

"I understand that, Dan... but let me just talk *around*

the subject a bit. Let me ask you a couple of questions, and if it's something you can't talk about, I'll ask a different question. For example, does don Fernando know Father Lopez? Are they friends?"

"They're closer than brothers. Yes, very good friends."

"And do you think that don Fernando thinks that Father Lopez is reliable, that Father Lopez is not off his rocker?" Ricardo asked

"I would say that Fernando trusts Father Lopez with his life, and that he thinks Father Lopez is completely sane."

"Are you aware of the story of the brujo's house being burned down, some fifteen years ago?" Ricardo asked.

"I'm aware of it, yes."

"Did that really happen?"

Dan just nodded his head yes.

"Who burned the house?" Ricardo asked.

"I can't talk about that," Dan said.

"Okay. Has don Fernandez ever seen the brujo himself?"

"Yes."

"What does he look like?"

"I asked him that. He said that the brujo was an old man, but not bent over like most old men around here. Stocky build, but not fat. Strong. Dark skin, white hair, white moustache."

Ricardo suddenly felt crestfallen. He realized that he was still clinging to the hope that the man at the bathhouse was not the brujo.

"Señores," said the man behind the counter, as he placed two plates of food on the counter.

"I'll get them," said Dan.

Dan got up and brought the two meals to the table, and then went back to get the two drinks. Ricardo could only pick at his lunch. He had lost his appetite.

"This is serious?" Dan suddenly asked.

"Yeah, I think so," Ricardo said. "Father Lopez says that this guy is stalking me."

"You've talked to Father Lopez?" Dan asked.

"Uh huh. I spent several hours with him yesterday."

"Can I tell don Fernando that?" Dan asked. "That might change his mind about letting me talk more with you."

"Sure... why not?" Ricardo said. He wasn't sure what he had hoped to learn from Dan, but nothing Dan had said had made him feel better. Dan seemed to sense this and after a few more minutes of silence, he said, "I didn't know this was serious, Ricardo. I'll talk to don Fernando again. I'll see what I can do."

"Thanks man," Ricardo said, "I appreciate it."

Ricardo thought it best not to press Dan anymore about don Fernando or the brujo. He only hoped that he had not opened a Pandora's Box by saying that Dan could tell don Fernando that he had talked to Father Lopez. If don Fernando was really as close as brothers with Father Lopez, who knows what Father Lopez might reveal about Ricardo to him? Ricardo had always kept his sexuality to himself—it was simply nobody's business but his own. But this was different. He simply hoped that Father Lopez would be discrete if don Fernando talked with him. Hell, he thought, it was such a small town anyway—who knew what all the locals really knew about the gringos? The fact that Jenny had told Father Lopez about Ricardo spoke volumes about who was loyal to whom. Blood was always thicker than water, he thought. There were things that gringos would never understand, never know, about Panamanians, about what they did: whom they talked with, what secrets they shared. Ricardo just had to hope for the best.

In the meantime, he changed the subject, and he and Dan talked about other things: Dan's new motorcycle; how Ted, Jenny's husband, was doing; local gossip; etc. Ricardo managed to finish most of his meal. Even though he had lost his appetite, he knew he needed to eat.

At the end of the meal, Ricardo thanked Dan and said he would talk to him soon. Dan looked a bit worried and said, "Yes... You take care, dude," as they said their goodbyes.

As he walked back to his apartment, Ricardo started to feel a bit angry. He was angry that Father Lopez just seemed to assume that he was done for; he was angry that don Fernando was being so secretive about what he knew about the brujo, if in fact he really did know anything; and he was angry that Dan was being so hush-hush about what don Fernando had told him. *Everyone's just trying to protect their little fucking corner of the world*, he thought to himself. *It's bullshit.*

One thought recurred to him as he was walking. He remembered Father Lopez saying that, despite all, the brujo was just a man and could be killed. Not that Ricardo was going to go to that length, but if the brujo was just a man, it meant he could be dealt with. He could be confronted; he could be tricked; and he could be stopped. Fuck Father Lopez. Fuck don Fernando. Fuck Dan. He was going to do something to protect himself.

By the time that Ricardo got back to his apartment, he was furious. He had to do something. He needed a plan, and he sat down at his writing desk with a pad of paper and began to make notes.

*   *   *

That night, Ricardo did not drink. He placed his gravity knife underneath his pillow and went to bed early. Having the knife within reach somehow made him feel better. He took off his clothes as he normally might do to go to bed, because he always slept naked. But on this night, he put on a t-shirt. It was an older t-shirt, a bit too tight to be comfortable. He did that on purpose because he didn't want to sleep soundly. He knew from experience that whenever he wore a t-shirt to bed, the constrictive cloth kept him from sleeping deeply, especially if he moved in his sleep. He lay down on his bed, covered himself with the thin blanket, closed his eyes and willed himself into that hypnagogic state right between sleep and wakefulness. He tried to float there as long as he could, holding his plan in mind, visualizing all the streets of Villa Rosario, sending out thoughts to the brujo, inviting him to come to him in his dreams, inviting him, inviting him...

And then... Ricardo found himself walking on the

outskirts of town on a dirt road. Behind him were the rolling fields that led to Villa Rosario. Up ahead the road angled sharply up into the hills. Ricardo started walking up the road, away from town. Up ahead was what looked like an old olive tree. But even in his dreaming state, Ricardo knew there were no olive trees in Villa Rosario. Maybe it was an apple tree, he thought. He looked at it. The brujo stepped out behind it. Ricardo felt afraid. He knew he was dreaming and tried to wake himself up. The scene did shift a bit, but then he was back on the road, still looking at the old tree. The brujo somehow had moved closer. Ricardo could see a blue glow around his pelvis, and then he suddenly was even closer, and Ricardo could see the electric blue semen spinning madly around his scrotum. The brujo reached down and unzipped his pants and took out his cock. It was dark and large. Ricardo tried to turn, to run away, but he felt something tight around his neck, and under his arms, and then briefly—just for a second—he realized that it was the t-shirt. And then he turned toward the brujo and said... or thought... but somehow conveyed the message: "I will only fuck you inside your house."

The brujo stepped back. Suddenly, Ricardo was awake.

"Fuck," he thought. He looked at the clock by the bed. One a.m. He lay there for a minute, feeling the urge to go back to sleep creep over him. "Goddamnit," he said out loud and threw the blanket off him and sat up. He grabbed his notebook by the bed and wrote quickly: "dirt road / sun to my right / olive tree / sharp hill in front". Then he got up and made a small pot of coffee.

He tried not to think. He didn't want to talk himself out of doing what he had planned to do. His body wanted desperately to go back to sleep, but he knew that deep sleep would leave him vulnerable. But if he drank a cup of strong coffee and then went back to sleep, the caffeine wouldn't kick in for another thirty minutes. Thus he would fall asleep, but after thirty minutes he would not be able to sleep deeply. He had to keep himself on track, and not talk himself out of this plan.

"La la la la," he sang to himself to keep his mind distracted as the coffee brewed. When a cup was ready, he poured it into a cup, added two large teaspoons of sugar and drank it down quickly. Then he turned off the lights and crawled back into bed and closed his eyes and tried to visualize the olive tree.

Other images filled his head. He thought of birds. Something was swirling. He felt a breeze. He looked up. The wind was blowing hard. To his left was a narrow road along the side of a cliff. He looked to his right. There was another road going the other way around the other side of this hill. He looked down and around. He was standing in the middle of a fork in the road. He turned and looked back down the road. Way in the distance was the town of Villa Rosario. And far below him, down the hill, Ricardo could see the olive tree. The road came up to this fork and went left or right. There was no one around him. He started walking to the left.

The sky was getting dark. He felt agitated, but he also felt excited. He knew that soon he would be sucking that large cock. Soon he would have it in his mouth, and maybe up his ass. He wanted it. He wanted to grab it and suck it and most of all he wanted to feel the blue semen shoot out. It had to shoot out or it would be no good. He wanted to feel it shoot out hard and hit the back of his throat, to make him gag with the amount of it, to make him swallow, not once but several times to get it all in. He wanted to take it all in. The more he walked, the more excited he became. He was walking faster now. Up ahead was a house, but Ricardo knew this was not the brujo's house. The windows had glass, and one window was broken. He kept walking. There was another house, almost a shanty. No lights were on, and the sky was dark now. Ricardo walked more. The road stopped. In front of him was a tiny house with lights on. There was no glass in the windows, just some type of oilcloth covering them from the inside. The front door was slightly ajar. His stomach hurt. He walked up to the house. A blue light shown from inside. His stomach hurt more. He put his hand out to touch the door.

He awoke. Light was coming into his bedroom. His stomach did hurt, something awful. He rubbed his eyes and looked at the clock. Six a.m. He reached over to his notepad and wrote: "wind / fork in road / olive tree below / go left / two houses / glass broken glass / oilcloth window / end of road." He put the notepad back on the table and just lay in bed. He felt like shit. But he knew where the brujo lived. Now he just had to find out where that olive tree was.

Chapter 14:   Rough Sketches

Ricardo wasn't much of a sketch artist, but he wanted to remember as much detail of the olive tree and the road as possible, so he took several sheets of paper out of his printer's paper tray and started to sketch the olive tree, the way it had looked when he first saw it. It had a thick trunk with gnarly roots going into the ground, and the branches, which hung low to the ground, all seemed to make right degree angles every foot or so. It had only a few small leaves on some of the branches. Ricardo had no idea what olive trees actually looked like. The most he could remember was that it was an old, possibly dead, tree with low-lying twisted limbs that jutted left and right, but he tried to draw it as best he could. The thing that seemed the most important to him was that he had seen the tree in the late afternoon and the sun was to his right above and behind the tree and the dirt road he was walking on was to the left. That gave him some orientation, he thought, some way to recognize the tree. Then he drew another picture of the fork in the road way up the hill—there wasn't much detail there, just a T-intersection against the side of a bare-rock hill, with one dirt road going left and the other one going right. Then on a third piece of paper he drew a sketch of the first two houses. He couldn't remember much about them except that one was to his right as he walked up the dirt road, butting up against the side of the hill. It had glass windows and one pane was busted out. The other house was nearby, farther up the dirt road but visible from the first house. It was on the left side of the dirt road, and the only thing Ricardo could remember about it was that it looked abandoned. He remembered there were no lights on, and he didn't think the windows had any glass in them.

Finally, on the last piece of paper, Ricardo tried to draw the brujo's house. It was on the right side of the road, against the rocky hill, out of sight of the other houses. He wasn't sure how much farther up the hill it was, nor could he remember much about it, except that it had a small wooded porch with one step. There was a door and a window to each side of the door. That was all Ricardo could remember. Then he went over to his desk and looked at the notes he had hastily written down just after waking, and he saw that he had written *oilcloth*. He had forgotten about that—the windows of the brujo's house did not have glass. Instead there was some thick dark oilcloth tacked up on the inside of the window that was fluttering in the breeze. Ricardo went back to his writing desk and added that to the drawing of the brujo's house. As he did that, another image suddenly came to mind. He remembered that to the left of the brujo's house there was a large shallow pit, about five feet deep and ten feet across. It looked like it had been dug out of the earth to be used as a landfill and seemed to have at least a foot of trash in it, old tires, branches, and garbage. In the dream, Ricardo had scarcely glanced at it when he was walking up to the house.

Ricardo couldn't remember much about the house. He thought it was a shanty, made of scrap wood. The roof was definitely scrap metal of different colors, hammered onto the top of the house, rattling in the wind.

He looked at his four drawings. That was all he could remember, but he was glad he had drawn them, because he knew how fast the details of any dream memory can evaporate into thin air. At least he had got these images down. He put the four drawings in a manila folder and thought about what he needed to do next. There were many dirt roads all around the outskirts of town—too many for him to walk to all of them. Ricardo had never owned a car in Panama. But now, for the first time, he needed to borrow one, or maybe rent one and drive around. Or maybe he could just hire a taxi for the day. But he would have to start off by finding that olive tree. He started doodling on a 3x5 card, drawing a small square to represent Villa Rosario then a small north-south arrow. Villa Rosario was laid out on a north-south grid, so that all the streets in the center of town, ran either north and south, or east and west. Like almost all of the old towns in Panama, this was because the Parque Central and Church were built first, and the center park of any town was always aligned north and south.

Then Ricardo drew a curved arrow over the town to represent the arc of the sun going from east to west. He drew a circle on the arc to represent where the sun was when he had seen the olive tree. At this point Ricardo was just doodling. He realized he was hungry and needed to eat some breakfast. He wondered what he had left in the refrigerator. Then he drew an X to represent where he must have been when he was standing at the fork in the road looking down at the town from up on the hill. Then it hit him. He had to have been south of the town. He had been looking down from a hill and the late afternoon sun was to the left in the sky. As he thought about it, the image of that view of the town that he had seen came back into focus in his mind. Yes, he had been standing at a fork in a dirt road, south of Villa Rosario, up in the hills, looking down upon the town. South. It fit the image that had just popped back into his mind. The brujo lived south of town, up in the hills. How could he get up those hills? There were no rent-a-car places in Villa Rosario. Dan had that motorcycle. Maybe Dan would let him borrow it. Ricardo thought back: he had had a motorbike years ago, but he realized that it had been over forty years ago, maybe longer. And he hadn't driven one since. Maybe he ought not to do that. His reflexes were not what they used to be. Maybe Dan could take him on the back of the bike. But he would decide later. Now, he needed to eat something.

*   *   *

Just as he was finishing breakfast out on the patio, his cell phone rang. He got up and went inside to answer it. It

121

was Dan.

"Hey," Dan said. "I hope I'm not calling too early."

"No, man. I was just finishing breakfast. What's up?"

"Well, turns out that don Fernando would like to talk with you after all. Do you have time today?"

"All I've got is time, Dan. Sure."

"Okay," Dan said. "Do you know where his office is?"

"It's the police station on the north corner of the park, isn't it?"

"Uh huh," said Dan. "I'll be there at one o'clock. Can you meet us then?"

"Sure," said Ricardo, then added, "And I'm glad you called for another reason. I need a favor later this afternoon if you've got some time."

Dan laughed. "Well, like you, my friend, all I've got is time. What is it?"

"I'll tell you later, after don Fernando."

"Okay. See you at one," Dan said and hung up.

Good, Ricardo thought. Maybe he'd learn something from don Fernando. He took his breakfast plate into the kitchen, washed it and put it in the dish rack, refilled his coffee, and went back out on his patio to think.

As a rational man, what was so frustrating to him was that he had no way to test anything that anyone was telling him. In fact, as a rational man, the whole affair was idiotic. All his rational brain could accept as fact was that some old stocky man in a gay bathhouse tried to make him suck his cock, and in trying to get away, he slipped and hit his head. *Everything else* was rumor and superstition. He had a few bad dreams—so what? The locals believed in witch doctors—so what? The local priest believed in witch doctors too—so what? Young people in the town moved away or disappeared and the local cop blamed the occult—and this was the same cop who had his job because supposedly he stood up to the occult. And here he was, trying to map out the location of some witch doctor based on a dream! Shit, he thought, he might as well be living in the Middle Ages... or in an insane asylum. As a rational man, this whole affair was ignorant village hysteria. And he was getting bamboozled by it.

But as an intuitive man, he knew there was a certain internal consistency to everything that had happened. He had been having dreams about the old man before anyone had told him about brujos. There was the consistency between what the brujo looked like in his dreams and the old man in the bathhouse. And then there was the fact that at least three people, Jenny, Father Lopez, and don Fernando all had similar views on the brujo... well, that remained to be seen regarding don Fernando. Ricardo made a mental note to test whether what don Fernando might tell him matched up with what Father Lopez had told him. Then there was the fact that the brujo came to him in the dream last night when Ricardo invited him to, just like Father Lopez said would happen. Then there was the consistency between how sexual the brujo had always been in his dreams with what both Jenny and Father Lopez had told him about the brujo and sex. He made another mental note to find a way to ask someone about the blue semen—maybe Jenny. Maybe that hooker who fled Jenny's had said something to Jenny about electric blue semen. He would have to find a way to ask Jenny that didn't suggest an answer. If Jenny volunteered to him that the girl had told her about blue semen or blue-anything in the brujo's pelvis, that would be another consistency. He didn't think he could ask Father Lopez about it, but maybe he could... Maybe the many young people who he had talked to over the years had said something.

But it was pointless to analyze it further. He had made his plan and he was going to stick to it. He would just have to push ahead and see what happened. Father Lopez had hinted that Ricardo could simply leave town, get beyond the brujo's range, but Ricardo had rejected that idea. He liked Villa Rosario, or at least, he had liked it very much until all this happened. But more importantly, he had nowhere else to go. There was nothing back in the States anymore, and he was tired of traveling to new places. He had spent all of his life traveling, he thought, from his birthplace in Spain to his paternal grandfather's farm in Virginia as a boy, and then back and forth to Spain, always being shuttled between relatives. And then as a young man, all over Europe, and then finally settling in the United States, and after years of traveling the different states, and a few rehab places, he had finally ended up in Hamburg, New York. When he got there, he thought he would stay, but of course that didn't happen. He kept moving. Was his whole life just one big long-distance marathon? Always running, always exiting, always moving away from somewhere? And over the years, one by one, losing all his family, and almost all his friends the further he went... It made him sad to think of it. When he had first come to Panama, he thought he could have two homes, one here and one back in the States, but it didn't turn out that way. Now, he felt that there truly was no place in the world where he belonged. It's people that create a feeling of belonging, he thought, and he had let them all slip away, and had ended up just another old man alone in another country. He still had Marta, of course. He would always have her because of their history together. But even she had become like a distant satellite, and their orbits only crossed once every year or maybe once every two years. Now with Carolina out of the picture, there simply was no one else left. Haley was gone, Eve was gone, Alison was gone, Cody was gone... All the men and women he had ever loved, or thought he could love, were gone down the tunnel of time. Another reason not to run from Villa Rosario, he thought. He would stay and see this brujo business to the bitter end.

*　　*　　*

At one o'clock, Ricardo met Dan outside of the small metal building that served as Villa Rosario's police station, and they went inside. Ricardo had only met and spoken with don Fernando once before, and that was many years ago, when Dan had introduced them at Ted's apartment complex, where Ricardo had first lived when he had moved to Villa Rosario. Ricardo had not particularly liked don Fernando back then. He didn't dislike him—it was just that don Fernando seemed a bit officious, a bit too self-important, somewhat of a control-freak, and not that bright, not unlike many overweight sheriffs in one-horse towns back in the

124

States. On the other hand, he was Dan's friend, and he had been the face of the law and order for many years in Villa Rosario and would probably hold that job until he retired or died.

Dan took Ricardo into don Fernando's office in the back of the building. The office was small for one person, making don Fernando look too big for the desk. There were two chairs in front of the desk, and Dan and Ricardo squeezed in and sat down. After exchanging greetings, don Fernando tried to get right to the point.

"Tell me everything you know about this brujo, don Ricardo," he said in Spanish.

But Ricardo was not wanting to let don Fernando control the meeting. Since his dream about the olive tree, it seemed to Ricardo that he might know a bit more than don Fernando did about the brujo, so Ricardo said nothing. He just stared at don Fernando. Ricardo had learned many years ago, as a lawyer, that the thing that unnerves people who want to be in control is silence. They are used to handling any reaction from an opponent, except silence. Besides, as a gringo, he could get away with more. So, Ricardo just smiled slightly, and picked a spot in the middle of don Fernando's forehead, right between his eyes, and just stared at it. That was another trick he had learned years ago: that if he focused on a spot to stare at in between the other person's eyes, he would not be subject to or influenced by their stare, while still giving the impression that he was looking them directly in the eyes. The slight smile was to appear friendly, of course.

Six or seven seconds of silence can be a very long time to a control-freak, and Ricardo could sense don Fernando shifting nervously. Finally don Fernando broke the silence. "Father Lopez is a good friend, and he has shared your situation with me."

"Then you know everything I know," Ricardo said.

"Well, for example, how many times did you dream about the brujo before he appeared?"

Ricardo leaned forward, forced himself to smile broadly, and said, "Does that really matter, señor? Unless of course, you didn't believe Father Lopez's word."

"Of course I believe Father Lopez! He is the grand-padre of our town."

"Good," said Ricardo, "then let's get to the point. Where does the brujo live?"

"Somewhere in the hills. We do not know exactly."

"But you have interviewed many people over the years?"

"Yes," said don Fernando, "many children."

"And some of them have described his house to you, correct?"

Ricardo could see a tiny movement as don Fernando's eyes widened for a split-second. Don Fernando did not know that Ricardo had deduced this. He nodded his head yes.

Ricardo reached into the manila folder he had brought, and carefully extracted just his sketch of the brujo's house. He placed it on the table and slid it towards don Fernando. This time he could see don Fernando's eyes widen and stay wide. He actually sensed don Fernando pushing back from the desk. Don Fernando looked at the drawing and then looked quickly at Ricardo.

"You have been there?" he blurted.

"No, but I saw it in a dream," Ricardo said.

Don Fernando seemed to let out a breath of air. "Good... if you had actually been there, he would have taken you." Then he leaned forward and studied the drawing. Ricardo could see his lips purse tighter. He looked up at Ricardo, then back at the drawing. He seemed to be thinking. Then he got up, went to an old metal file cabinet in the corner, opened the second drawer, and took out a thick bundle of file folders tied with string. He placed it on his desk, untied the string and pulled out a tattered tan folder, opened it and spread out three pieces of paper in front of Ricardo. One was a watercolor, one appeared to be a crude map, and the third was a pencil drawing.

"These were done by three different children, in different years," don Fernando said. "They each told me they saw it in a dream... and each of them, within a week... were gone."

Ricardo leaned forward to look at the papers. They were primitive, as children's drawings are, but each showed three houses, two on one side of a road, one on the other. The watercolor was the best drawing, and it showed a tiny porch on the last house, with two lines supporting a roof over the porch. Brown lines dipped to the left of the house, suggesting a large ditch. The pencil drawing was a primitive stick drawing, showing three shacks, but the map showed what looked to be a child's representation of a hill behind the houses. They each, crudely, matched Ricardo's drawing.

"Did these children say which house was the brujo's house?" Ricardo asked.

Don Fernando just pointed to the last house on the map drawing.

Ricardo nodded, then sat back in his chair, crossed his arms and thought for a bit. Then he asked, "Don Fernando, did any of these children say that there was any color associated with the brujo?"

"This girl," don Fernando said, "pointing at the watercolor. She was older and outspoken, and she had brothers. She said he had blue privates."

Dan, who had remained quiet this whole time, leaned in to look at the drawings, then asked, "Ricardo, do you know where this house is?"

"Sort of... We'd have to drive around until I saw some landmarks."

"Tell us, and don Fernando can send someone out to look."

"No, Dan. I want to be there. If he has a car, we can go driving right now. I have a sense of the direction, but we would need to drive around a bit."

Ricardo glanced up to the wall to the right of don Fernando's desk. There was a large map of Villa Rosario. Ricardo had noticed it when they first walked in, but now he looked at it carefully. It had more detail than he first realized, showing the topological lay of the land surrounding the town, including dotted lines for dirt roads and trails. Like many small towns in Panama that were surrounded by hills, there were a whole spider's web of dirt roads and paths that blossomed out from the town up to the hills and to the hundreds of poor people who lived in shacks up in those hills.

Ricardo stood up and examined the map carefully, looking at the roads that led out towards the south. Dan was asking don Fernando whether there was a car available, and don Fernando got on the telephone.

There were several dotted lines that led south, and up to the hills, but one line seemed to meander through a lowland first, before heading up.

Don Fernando got off the phone, and nodded to Dan. "We have a car available," Dan said.

Ricardo had a moment of doubt and said, "This may be a wild goose chase, Dan... but yes, let's go." He pointed to the dotted line on the map that he had been looking at, and said to don Fernando, "Can we drive down this road?"

"Sí," said don Fernando. He opened the top drawer to his desk, took out a gun with a clip-on holster and attached it to his belt.

Ricardo doubted that a gun would be necessary, but said nothing, and the three men filed out of the office.

*   *   *

The dirt road south of town did meander through fields, none of which looked familiar to Ricardo. He was sitting in front, with Dan in back. Don Fernando was driving the old police car. They drove for twenty minutes away from town. The rocky dirt road made it impossible to go faster than ten or fifteen miles an hour. Clouds of dust rose up from the rear of the car. Rocky hills loomed ahead. These were the steepest hills surrounding Villa Rosario, much more perpendicular and desolate than the hills that Ricardo had traveled with Marco to get to Hotel de Sevilla. Ricardo wondered if they were volcanic hills, maybe more recent, geologically speaking, than the other hills around the town.

"Are you sure this is the right road, señor?" don Fernando asked as they hit another jarring bump in the road.

"No," said Ricardo, "but keep going."

The road angled left gently then made a sudden right angle.

"Wait! Stop the car!" Ricardo suddenly said.

There was the tree. Ricardo got out and ran up the road to it, followed by don Fernando and Dan. Ricardo stopped about twenty feet from the tree and just stared at it. It wasn't an olive tree... maybe an old dead apple tree, he thought. But it was definitely the large gnarly trunk with forked branches that he had seen in the dream. This was it. He looked up the road. It went straight to the hill and then up the hill. Dan ran up next to Ricardo, followed by don Fernando, huffing and trying to catch his breath.

"Recognize this?" Dan asked.

"Yes, very vividly. This is where I saw him. He stepped out from behind that tree," Ricardo said.

"Ayúdanos, Dios," don Fernando said between gasps for air.

"The road goes up that hill to a T-intersection against the cliff. He lives somewhere down the left road," Ricardo said. "Let's go."

"No, no, señor," don Fernando said. "Not in the police car. He will see us. We need more men. Plus, we need to come at night. He can only appear at night. In the day, he is invisible."

"Nonsense!" Ricardo said. "I've seen him during the day! He's just a man. Let's just go up there and confront him, see what's he's doing! C'mon!"

"No señor. No," don Fernando said. His voice was firm.

Ricardo looked at Dan. Dan said, in English, so that don Fernando wouldn't understand, "He's the law, dude. Plus, it's his car. Let the Panamanians handle this."

"Like they did the last time?" Ricardo shot back. Then he looked at Dan and don Fernando, shook his head, said "Fuck!" and walked back to the car. He had fucked up. He should not have told them where the house was. He should have just told them to drive more. He was mad at himself for getting excited about finding the tree and not thinking strategically. He got into the back seat of the car. Dan got into the front, and don Fernando got into the driver's side, started the car up, and began to turn it around.

On the way back to town, Ricardo sat silently, but he was actively watching the route, making mental notes of the twists and turns, of how far the distance actually was. He wondered how difficult the terrain would be at night. He wondered if he could walk this far. But mostly, he wondered how much further up the hill the three houses actually were. He was so pissed that he didn't trick them into going further. The brujo's house could be just up the hill a bit, or it could be miles up the hill. He just didn't know, and he wouldn't know until he went there himself. But at the moment there was nothing else he could do. He had played this hand as far as it went. Dan was obviously too tight with don Fernando for Ricardo to ask to borrow his motorcycle or to ask for a ride. Ricardo knew he needed to rethink his plan. He would have to go back to his apartment, regroup, and come up with some alternatives.

Back in town, don Ricardo parked the car in front of the police station. Ricardo had decided to play along, and when they were out of the car, he walked up to don Fernando and said, "Don Fernando, I will leave this matter in your capable hands. I got too excited back there. You have the experience to handle this brujo. I may leave town for a while, but Dan knows how to get in touch with me. Thank you for all your help."

"No, no, señor Ricardo, thank *you*. This is the first break we've had in years."

Then turning to Dan, Ricardo just said, "Keep me posted, man."

Dan looked at him, squinted a little, but nodded his head, and said, "Sure, man. Will do. You stay in touch too."

"Yup," Ricardo said, and turned to walk home, leaving Dan with don Fernando.

Chapter 15:   Taxi

The next morning after breakfast, Ricardo walked down to the Parque Central. At the west end of the park was a large tree whose branches overhung the street, casting shadows on both the sidewalk and street. This is where the local taxi drivers parked their cars and waited for fares. The drivers would all sit on the gray concrete benches that lined the park and talk, or smoke, and wait. There was no dispatch system in Villa Rosario, no line of taxis waiting to take fares in order. In fact, there were no regular taxis. All of the taxis were unmarked gypsy cabs. If one wanted a cab, one would simply walk to this corner and wave to their favorite driver who would get up and point to whatever car he was driving that day.

Everyone in town had a favorite taxi driver, like an adopted son. It was a system that worked well, because the driver had an incentive to keep a loyal customer, and so would do extra things, like help carry the groceries into the house. The customers also had an incentive to keep the driver happy, because if a customer, for example, needed a midnight ride to the hospital in La Chorrera, he knew he could call his favorite driver at home in the middle of the night, rouse him from sleep, and get a ride quickly.

Ricardo's favorite driver was a man named Minor. As Ricardo walked up to the taxi corner, he saw Minor sitting in his usual seat on the concrete bench closest to the corner, talking to another taxi driver. Ricardo waved at Minor, and Minor stood up to greet him and they both walked to Minor's car, an old beat-up Hyundai.

"Minor, I want to take a little drive in the county, nowhere special, just drive around a bit," Ricardo said in Spanish as he got into the front passenger seat of Minor's taxi.

"Any place you want, señor," Minor replied. Unlike most Panamanians, Ricardo always tipped Minor, so he was glad to take Ricardo anywhere, anytime.

"Let's just head south, out of town," Ricardo said. "I just want to enjoy the morning and see places I haven't seen before."

Ricardo knew that taxi drivers all talked, so he didn't want to give the impression that he was going anywhere specific. He directed Minor up and down various roads that led out of town, and they chatted about the various neighborhoods, who lived there, what the local gossip was, etc. But finally they ended up at the road that Ricardo knew would take them to the old tree.

"Where does this road lead, Minor?" Ricardo asked.

"Nowhere, señor. It just goes up into the hills where renegades and squatters live."

"Hmm... you know, a friend of mine told me that there was a roadside stand down one of these roads where someone sells honey. I think it might be this road."

"I do not think so, señor," Minor replied.

"Well, I don't know, Minor, but I've never been down here before, so let's drive a ways and see what's down there."

"Sí señor."

And so Minor's old taxi made its way slowly down the rocky dirt road, avoiding most of the potholes and large chunks of rock. At several points, Minor had to drive off the road to avoid big rocks. Eventually they came to the curve in the road which led to the old tree. Ricardo stared at it as they slowly drove past it.

"Minor, what kind of tree is that?" he asked.

"It is a fig tree, señor," Minor replied.

"A fig tree?" Ricardo exclaimed.

"Sí, an old dead fig tree, very old, maybe 100 years, I don't know. Back when all this was jungle, before the farms, there were many fig trees. But now, no more."

"I've never seen a fig tree so big. Does it have a name?" Ricardo asked.

"It is called a Strangler Fig, señor."

"Really? Do you know why?"

"Because in ancient times, the brujos would inhabit the trees at night and then lure people to the woods, and when the people got close to the tree, the brujos would wrap their limbs around them so tight to strangle them and then grow around them all night so in the morning no one could find their bodies. That is why the trunks swell so wide—they are full of bodies."

"Really? How would the brujos lure people to the woods?" Ricardo asked.

"With dreams," Minor said.

"And do you believe that actually happened?"

Minor took a quick look at Ricardo. "Of course not, señor. I am an educated man. But you asked why it was called that. Do you want me to keep going down this road? I do not think there is any honey down here."

"Maybe just a little further, Minor... just to see where it goes."

Minor's taxi made its bumpy way past the old tree for about a mile until it came to the large rocky hill that loomed over the valley. The dirt road angled steeply up the hill.

"What's up this hill, Minor?" Ricardo asked.

"Squatters and bandits, señor. I do not know. I've never gone up there."

"Never in your whole life?" Ricardo asked.

"No señor, never. There is never a reason to go to the bad lands."

"Huh. Well, I tell you what, Minor. I'm curious. Let's just go up a bit," Ricardo said.

Minor looked worried. He looked at the steep incline, and then back at Ricardo.

"Just a little ways, Minor, then we can go back," Ricardo said, to reassure Minor.

"Okay, señor. I will try."

Minor's old Hyundai struggled up the steep road that wrapped around the bottom part of the hill. About 1000 feet further, the road came to the T-intersection that Ricardo recognized.

"Hang on a second here, Minor," Ricardo said. Minor stopped the car, and Ricardo jumped out and looked around. Yes, this was the place. He felt sure that it wasn't just a fork in the road that resembled his dream—this *was* the exact place he had been at in his dream. The rocky cliff, the foliage, the angle of the road all matched. Ricardo peered up the road to the left. It went up at even a steeper angle. He climbed back into Minor's taxi.

"Can we go to the left, Minor?" Ricardo asked.

"No, señor, I am sorry. This old car will not make it," Minor said.

"Really?" Ricardo asked, "you don't think so?"

"No, señor. I know this car. She will die up there, and we do not want to be stranded up here."

Ricardo thought for a second. He took in the car's torn and faded interior—it *was* a very old car. Perhaps Minor was right. He had not even brought water, and the morning was already hot.

"Okay, Minor," Ricardo said, "you are right. We've done enough this morning. Let's go back."

"Thank you, señor," Minor said in a relieved tone. He managed to turn the car around by entering the intersection to the left and backing up a bit to turn around and go back down the steep hill.

"So, you think there's just squatters up there?" Ricardo asked.

"Yes, señor, everyone knows that," Minor replied.

"Well, who owns these hills?"

"Who knows? Originally they belonged to the Cuevas. Many still live up there," Minor said.

"What? Cuevas? Minor, no... I mean, I thought the Cuevas were all wiped out by the Spaniards in, like, the 1600's. And besides, they didn't live in this area. They lived far east of here, near the Colombian border."

Minor just shrugged. "I only know what my grandfather told me, señor: that when the Spaniards came, the Cuevas fought them hard, but the Spaniards had guns.

So, the Cuevas made peace with the Chocós, and both groups moved west to settle in these hills to get away from all foreigners. Which is why to this day, we never see them. They keep to themselves and to the old ways of the indigenous ones. Sometimes local men who cannot find wives here will go up to join them, to find a wife, but I don't know if they find wives or if the Cuevas kill them. But they never come back. I am glad I found a wife here in town, señor."

"Let me ask you this, Minor. If they're just squatting on the land, why doesn't the government send police or the army up there to... well, to see what's going on?"

Minor gave a little laugh. "They would be killed, señor. Besides, you've lived here long enough to know we never do anything that isn't necessary. The squatters don't bother anyone. Why go up there?"

Ricardo sat back and thought for the remainder of the trip back to town. He remembered reading about the Cuevas when he first came to Panama. A fierce tribe, supposedly wiped out by the Spaniards and by disease... at least that's what the history books said. But over the years, he had learned to take history books with a grain of salt. They were all just codified myths, some type of culturally agreed upon reality of what had happened in the past, usually used to justify the present. As such, they were neither more nor less reliable than the oral histories that were handed down to the actual descendants of the area.

But he was going to have to rethink his plan. He wanted to get up to the brujo's house somehow. He wasn't sure what he was going to do when he got there, but he was going to somehow take care of this problem. He decided to call Dan when he got back to his apartment—to see what don Fernando was doing. Maybe don Fernando was assembling a team to go up there, and Ricardo could join them.

Minor's cab reached the outskirts of town. The road, though still dirt, was at least smooth and devoid of rocks. Ricardo heard Minor breathe a sigh of relief, and Ricardo resolved to give him an extra tip for the morning's drive.

Chapter 16:   Nothing Is What It Appears

After Minor dropped him off at his apartment, Ricardo called Dan.

"Ah," Dan said when he heard Ricardo's voice, "you haven't left town after all."

"No," Ricardo said. "I still might, but I'm here today. But I wanted to call and see when don Fernando is going back to find the brujo's house. Do you think he might do that today?"

"It won't be today," Dan said. "He's still trying to round up enough people and come up with a plan."

"Jeez, Dan," Ricardo exclaimed. "How many people does it take to knock on some guy's door and see what he's up to?"

Dan just laughed. "This ain't the States, dude. You gotta give don Fernando time to do it his way."

"Alright Dan, alright, but do me a favor. I want to be there when he goes there. Can you find out when he's going and see if I can come along? I've got to see if this guy is the same guy I saw or not. I mean, what if I'm wrong? I don't want to accuse some old farmer based on some kooky dream I had."

"But you said you actually saw him in La Chorrera," Dan said.

"Yes, I saw him. That is, I saw someone who matched the person I saw in my dream. But I didn't see him at his house—I only saw that in my dream. I have to make sure that the guy I saw in La Chorrera actually lives in that house."

"Okay, okay, I'll tell don Fernando you want to be

there," Dan said, then added, "Listen Ricardo, really, you need to let don Fernando handle this. Don't try and go there yourself—this is an old fight and you don't want to get caught in the crossfire. I'll try and convince don Fernando to include you. But be patient."

"Okay Dan, I'll try. Just let me know what he says."

"I will."

*   *   *

But the next day, Ricardo just got the same response. Dan simply said that don Fernando wasn't going up the hill that day, either. He said he had relayed Ricardo's request to don Fernando, and don Fernando promised he would think about it and let Dan know whether it would be appropriate to allow Ricardo to be there. Dan promised to call Ricardo as soon as he heard something.

*   *   *

Ricardo heard nothing from Dan on the third day. All day long he debated whether he should call Dan, but kept telling himself that he shouldn't appear too eager, so he didn't call.

*   *   *

The fourth day also passed with no call from Dan. Maybe, he thought to himself, maybe if he had more information to take to don Fernando, he could wrangle another trip up the hill. So that afternoon he decided he would take a nap and try and see if he could dream more about the brujo's house—about how far up the hill it was from the fork in the road, and if there were any other landmarks he could use to find his way there. He lay down, closed his eyes, and tried to visualize the old tree. He put himself on the road, looking at the tree, and tried to imagine the breeze moving the branches, tried to imagine the sound of the dead twigs rubbing against each other, tried to recreate the smell

of the dusty road and the feel of the day warming up. He was
hoping the brujo would appear from behind the tree, and he
planned to reiterate that he would come to the brujo's house
if the brujo would show him the exact route... He replayed
the scene over and over in his mind, but after thirty minutes
of lying there, he gave up. His mind was too agitated, and his
body too frustrated, to sleep. He got up. It was too late in the
day to heat up more coffee, and too early in the afternoon to
drink, but he poured himself a small glass of Sangría anyway
and went out to the balcony to think and wait for the sunset.

*　　*　　*

By the afternoon of the fifth day, Ricardo was feeling
desperate. *This is so Panama,* Ricardo thought to himself.
*Nothing happens fast; nothing happens easy; and nothing
ever happens.* The more he thought about it, the more he
realized that don Fernando might never go up to the brujo's
house, because there really was no benefit for him. His police
job was created and maintained by the myth of the magical
threat that loomed outside of the city. If he went there and
there was just some old feeble squatter there, word might
get around... it might undermine his authority in this two-
bit town. Don Fernando wasn't going to jeopardize his job
just because some gringo had a dream. And while Dan was
Ricardo's friend, Dan wasn't going to bypass don Fernando
to help Ricardo. For whatever reason, Dan was always one
hundred percent loyal to don Fernando. Ricardo had always
suspected that the two had some illegal side business
together, some kind of deal that kept them locked into each
other. But he didn't know what it was. Villa Rosario didn't
really seem to have any organized crime. It was too small.

Ricardo sat out on his balcony and thought about
all this. He went back to his original plan. If don Fernando
wasn't going to investigate this brujo's house—and it was
clear that he wasn't—then Ricardo would simply have to do
it himself. But how? He couldn't walk from town. He couldn't
borrow Dan's motorcycle, because Dan would know what
he was up to and refuse him. Minor's car wouldn't make it

up the hill. He thought about having Minor take him to the fork in the road and wait for him while he walked up the hill, but he still didn't know how far up the hill the brujo's house was. Plus he didn't want to let Minor know that he had a particular destination. He wondered if he had been foolish in even having Minor drive him out to the tree. He had tried to make it appear random, but even so, word might have gotten back to don Fernando. No... if Ricardo was going to go out to the hill, he needed a car, and he needed to go alone.

Then he suddenly thought maybe he could borrow Miguel's car. Why hadn't he thought of that before? Miguel had that little Suzuki car. It wasn't new, but it wasn't as old as Minor's taxi. He had never asked Miguel to borrow the car before, but he thought Miguel would let him. And Miguel wouldn't be interrogating him about why he needed it. Yes! He would see if he could borrow Miguel's car.

He checked his watch. Miguel might be at the restaurant now, getting ready to open for dinner. He went inside and dialed the restaurant.

"Miguel, this is Ricardo," he said when the waiter who answered the phone brought Miguel to the phone.

"Ah, hola mi amigo," said Miguel. "¿Qué pasa?"

"Listen, my friend, I have a huge favor to ask," said Ricardo, "a really big favor."

"Yes?"

"Can I borrow your car tomorrow, just for a few hours? I have some errands to run out of town."

There was a short pause on the line, then Miguel asked, "Do you have a Panamanian driver's license?"

"Well... no," Ricardo said.

"Do you have any insurance?"

"Ah... no."

"Have you ever driven a car in Panama before?"

"No."

"Is it for anything illegal?"

"No, no, of course not, Miguel."

"Okay, you can borrow it. I need it in the morning, but if you come to the restaurant at one o'clock tomorrow, you can borrow it. You need to bring it back to the restaurant by nine, so I can get home."

"Miguel, thank you so much," Ricardo said, "I will take good care of it."

For the first time in five days, Ricardo began to relax. His plan, as such, wasn't much—he would drive up the hill, see if he could find that house, and if he could, he would knock on the door, and if the brujo answered, Ricardo would yell at him and act out of control. If it's one thing that Panamanians hate, it's out of control angry gringos. The Panamanian culture avoids conflict, and when gringos get loud and angry, it scares them. Ricardo thought it might work.

Besides, he didn't have a better plan.

*　　*　　*

It was later that same night. Ricardo was getting ready for bed. He had sat out on his balcony with his Sangría for a while, as was his custom, watching the stars come out. But now he had come inside, closed and locked his door, washed his wine glass out, brushed his teeth and washed his face, and was just getting ready to get undressed when he heard a knock on his door. It startled him because he never got visitors at his apartment. He pulled aside the vertical blinds on his front window and looked out to his balcony. It was Marco! Ricardo couldn't believe it. Marco had never been to his apartment before. In fact, Ricardo couldn't even remember if he had ever told Marco where he lived, but it was a small town, and Marco must have asked around. Ricardo unlocked and opened the wooden door quickly and looked at him. Marco just smiled.

"Come in, come in Marco," Ricardo said as he pushed open the screen door. "When did you get to town?"

"Just tonight," Marco replied. His voice sounded hoarse. He stepped inside. Ricardo stepped back, leaving the front door open, and looked at Marco. He looked the same, but different. Then Marco said, "I had to see you," and stepped closer to Ricardo, leaned in, and kissed him. This took Ricardo by surprise, but he kissed Marco back and reached both hands up to hold Marco's shoulders. The material of his shirt felt rough. Marco put one hand around Ricardo's waist and reached down with his other hand and rubbed the front of Ricardo's pants. He was kissing Ricardo hard and pushing his tongue into Ricardo's mouth to suck. Ricardo wasn't used to Marco being this aggressive. His head was swirling with questions, but he pushed them all aside. Sex always pushes everything aside. Ricardo wrapped his mouth around Marco's tongue and sucked it gladly, pushing his face harder into Marco's to get even more of that tongue into his mouth. Marco was rubbing the front of Ricardo's pants faster, and Ricardo was getting hard. He reached his right hand down to Marco's pants and rubbed him. Marco was already hard. Marco started walking Ricardo backwards, still kissing him, backing him up towards the corner of his little studio apartment where his bed was. By the time they got to the bed, Marco had unbuckled Ricardo's belt and unzipped the zipper. Ricardo pulled his head away, took a gasp of air and said, "Wait Marco, wait..." but Marco reached down with both hands and pulled Ricardo's pants and underwear down to his knees and pushed Ricardo backwards so he fell on the bed. Marco went down on Ricardo, taking his cock into his mouth, sucking him up and down, running his tongue around Ricardo's shaft. He used his hands to pull Ricardo's pants past his knees and off onto the floor. Ricardo had one hand on the top of Marco's head and the other arm thrown over his eyes blocking out the light so he could just feel Marco sucking him. Everything was happening so fast. Then Marco grabbed both of Ricardo's legs just behind the knees with both his hands and pushed both legs up towards Ricardo's head, bending Ricardo's pelvis up. Marco held both of Ricardo's legs up in the air with his hands and lowered his head to find Ricardo's asshole with his mouth. He probed Ricardo's asshole with his wet tongue, running the point around the asshole and pushing into it as hard as he could. Ricardo was in ecstasy. There is nothing like being enthusiastically rimmed and Marco was being very enthusiastic, almost violent. Marco pulled one hand down, placed his finger in his mouth to get it wet, and forced it into

Ricardo's asshole.

"Jesus fucking Christ, Marco, Jesus," was all Ricardo could say. He heard Marco spit on his finger a few times and shove it further up Ricardo's asshole each time. Then Marco took both of Ricardo's balls into his mouth and sucked and pulled them, then went back to sucking Ricardo's cock while he shoved his finger in and out of Ricardo's asshole.

Suddenly, Marco moved up on top of Ricardo. Ricardo had not seen him take off his pants, but they were off. Marco's cock was erect and right at Ricardo's mouth. Ricardo opened his mouth and Marco shoved his cock in. Marco had one hand behind Ricardo's head and used the other hand on the bed to brace himself. He began to fuck Ricardo's mouth. Ricardo sucked as best he could, but Marco was holding Ricardo's head still and just fucking his mouth in and out, harder and harder. Each time he thrust in, Ricardo almost gagged as the cock went further and further down his throat. He could feel the smooth shaft and the large head of Marco's cock as it moved in and out. Marco was simply taking him, fucking his face. Ricardo couldn't have moved if he wanted to, the way that Marco's legs were pinning him to the bed.

Ricardo looked up at Marco's face. He wanted to see Marco's face, to see if Marco was looking at him or whether his eyes were closed. But Marco's face began to change. Ricardo blinked hard twice and looked again. Marco's face was transforming, changing shape the harder he fucked Ricardo's face. And his cock seemed to be getting thicker, pushing against the sides of Ricardo's mouth. Ricardo was starting to gag. He looked again at Marco, but it wasn't Marco anymore. It was someone else. Then Ricardo saw clearly. It was the brujo, big and dark skinned, his fat body holding Ricardo down, fucking him, fucking him hard, raping his mouth. Ricardo started to fight but it was no use. The brujo's massive hand held Ricardo's head in a vice grip, and the weight of the brujo's body made movement impossible. The brujo's cock had forced Ricardo's jaw so wide open and was so far down his throat to make biting down impossible. Ricardo looked up in horror at the brujo's face. There was only a look of determination. His eyes were cold and staring straight ahead. His mouth was tight. Ricardo began beating on the brujo's thighs, punching him in the sides of his stomach, but it was like hitting sandbags. The brujo kept fucking, thrusting in and out.

Suddenly the brujo came. Ricardo could feel the brujo's cock lock up and then felt a stream of hot cum shoot out and hit the back of his throat. His throat was filling up with cum, running out of the corners of his mouth. A huge amount of cum. The brujo straightened up, and reached down with his other hand and squeezed Ricardo's nostrils closed so that Ricardo couldn't breathe and had to swallow the cum. The brujo thrust three more times. Ricardo started seeing stars. He was suffocating and losing consciousness. One, two, three hard squirts of cum, then a pause and then the brujo thrust hard one more time for a last squirt and released Ricardo's nose, and fell off of him. Ricardo rolled to the side, gasping for air, coughing and spitting out gobs of acrid cum. He couldn't get enough air in for the coughing. He coughed and spit out more cum. Suddenly he felt the impact—no pain, just the impact—of the brujo's fist hard against the back of his head, and everything went black.

*　　*　　*

When he came to, it was the next morning. He was lying in his bed, under the covers. He looked around. Light filled his little apartment. He moved his arms and legs, and then realized he had all his clothes on. He lifted the covers and looked. His pants were on, the belt buckled. His shirt was on and buttoned up. Even his socks were on. He blinked and moved his head around and wet his lips. He couldn't taste any cum aftertaste, and the back of his head where he had been hit didn't hurt.

He sat up in bed and moved his shoulders. Nothing hurt. Was it a dream? Did he drink too much Sangría and pass out? Had he just crawled into bed drunk and gone to sleep? Could that be? He had never had such a violent dream before. He threw the covers off and was just starting to get

144

out of bed when he looked over at the door. It was open. A bolt of fear hit him. One thing he would never do, drunk or sober, was leave his door open at night. He remembered closing it. He remembered locking it. He had only opened it when he heard the knock at the door. He felt his mouth again, running his tongue around the inside of his lips, moving his jaw, opening and closing his mouth. Something had definitely happened. The muscles of his jaw and mouth felt abused, the way he felt after leaving the dentist, having had to hold his mouth open for too long. He jumped up and went to the bathroom and looked at the mirror. His hair was mussed, but no more than usual in the morning. But he could see the tinge of rawness around his lips, from kissing and sucking. Still, there was no weird taste in his mouth. He walked back into the room and over to the open door. There was his patio, looking normal. He looked over to his little kitchen. Everything looked normal. Suddenly he panicked and ran to his nightstand and opened the drawer where he kept his wallet. It was there. All his money, his identification, and credit cards were still there. He closed the drawer and looked around. *Maybe I'm losing my mind*, he thought. He walked back over to the open door and closed it. There were his house keys, in the back of the door lock, exactly where he kept them every night after closing his door and locking the deadbolt. The only way they would have been there was if he had locked his door last night, but then opened it when Marco—or the brujo—knocked. He only put them in the deadbolt lock to either lock or unlock the door. He never would just leave them there with the door open.

Slowly the reality of what had happened began to sink in on him. He went to the bathroom and threw up, and then began to cry.

Chapter 17:   Perdition

The Ricardo who appeared at Miguel's restaurant that afternoon was not the same man who had telephoned Miguel the day before. The man who walked from the La Chorrera bus stop to Miguel's restaurant had the walk of a man on a mission... a mission of revenge. It is not the steps that mark such a walk; rather, it is the eyes—eyes that are no longer interested in taking in any of the visual forms that swirl around them, for they are eyes that only see one image, the target of revenge.

There was no doubt in Ricardo's mind anymore. The brujo had transformed himself into Marco, had come to Ricardo's house, and had raped him, forcing him to swallow that semen, to eat that ejaculate, to taste that viscous fluid that had originated deep in the brujo's seminal vesicles, prostate, and testicles, and to take that cum all the way down his throat into his stomach and make it part of Ricardo's body. It was not a question of magic anymore—it was real, it had happened. And now the only thing in Ricardo's mind was revenge.

Miguel noticed it right away. Ricardo did not stop at the dining area and ask for Miguel as he might have in the past. Instead, he walked straight back into the kitchen where Miguel was slicing tomatoes. Miguel was startled.

"Are you okay, amigo?" he asked Ricardo.

"I'm fine Miguel, but I'm in a bit of a hurry. Can I borrow the keys?"

"Of course, my friend," Miguel said and reached into his pocket. Then he frowned. "Oh wait, they are in my office.

Just a minute." And Miguel walked into the other room.

Ricardo looked around the well-organized kitchen. Two other workers were across the room, also chopping vegetables, their backs to Ricardo. Ricardo looked over at the tomato that Ricardo had been working on. Bright red slices lay on the cutting board beside the knife, its blade wet with tomato juice. Ricardo looked at the wooden block next the cutting board that held several other knives. Knives, he thought... He patted his pocket. He had not brought his gravity knife. He walked over and pulled out a large steak knife with a six-inch blade from the cutting block. It was an old knife with a worn wooden handle, but the edge was razor sharp. Miguel walked back into the room.

"Here are the keys, my friend," he said holding them out to Ricardo. "You know the car—it is parked in the lot in the back."

Ricardo reached out with his right hand and took the keys, still holding the knife in his left hand.

"Thanks, Miguel, I owe you."

He stuck the keys in his pocket and turned his attention back to the knife, feeling its weight, feeling how well the handle fit his hand.

"Where did you get this knife, Miguel?"

"You like it? It's very old, belonged to my father. It's hand-made. He made all of his knives himself."

"It's very nice... Can I borrow it?"

Miguel squinted just a bit and looked at Ricardo.

"You did tell me that you're not doing anything illegal, right?"

"Of course not, Miguel. I just want to show it to a friend of mine. I'll bring it back tonight with the car, I promise."

Miguel pursed his lips, paused, but then said, "Okay, my friend. Just be careful, it's very sharp. Here, let me find a sheath for it."

Miguel rummaged through two of the kitchen drawers until he found a black leather sheath. "This should work," he said, and handed it to Ricardo. Ricardo slid the knife into the scabbard. "Yes, that's good, Miguel, it fits. Thank you, my friend. I have to go now." And Ricardo turned and walked out. Miguel watched him leave, shook his head, but then returned to his tomato slicing.

Ricardo found the car in the back lot and got inside. The sun was high in the sky and the interior of the car was hot. Ricardo did not care. He turned the engine on and pulled out of the lot and headed for Villa Rosario.

Revenge is the root of all justice and the root of all evil. As Ricardo drove the route to Villa Rosario that he knew so well from the many bus rides he had taken, his mind was focused on one singularity—finding the brujo and killing him. There was no thinking, no processing, no consideration of alternatives or plans. There was just pure intention, completely oblivious to any consequences. He drove the forty minutes back to Villa Rosario, through the town, and headed south towards the old tree. He had to take the dirt road slower than he wanted, but he still drove faster than either don Fernando or Minor had. The bouncing rattled his bones. He had taken the sheathed knife and stuck it under his belt in the small of his back. It hurt his back every time he hit a rock or pothole, but he did not want to take it out and place it on the seat next to him. The pain only focused his intention more.

He passed the old tree without looking at it or slowing down and continued down the road toward the base of the rocky hill. At the hill, he began to drive the steep climb up, never getting out of first gear. At the fork in the road, he turned left and proceeded up a steeper dirt road.

At this point his eyes began to focus on his surroundings. This part of the journey was new to him. He had seen the fork in the road, and he had seen the brujo's house, but he had never seen the distance or the route between the two. The car was going slowly up the road, but Ricardo slowed down even more, looking left and right, trying to find something familiar.

The road was getting steeper as it angled higher up the hill. Ricardo wondered how he would get back down—there was no room to turn around. But he pushed on. Five more minutes, then another five, and then another five...

Ricardo began to wonder again if he was crazy, lost, or both... Then, at last, the road seemed to level out, curved slightly around the mountain... and there was a house he recognized on the right, with broken glass windows... and then the house on the left, the one that looked abandoned... and then the road curved more... Ricardo drove slowly around the bend, out of sight of the first two houses... and then he saw it, the brujo's house, with the oilcloth hanging in the windows, fluttering in the breeze. Ricardo gunned the engine, sped right up to the house, stopped the car, and jumped out. He wasn't trying to be stealthy. He didn't care who saw him. He just wanted revenge. He bounded up the wooden steps to the porch, lifted his right knee up and gave the front door a violent front kick with the bottom of his foot. There was a huge bang as the wooden latch on the inside shattered and the door burst open. Ricardo stepped inside.

The inside was completely dark except for the shaft of light from the open door which didn't seem to reflect or illuminate anything beyond the black floor where it hit. Instantly Ricardo knew why the oilcloth was tacked up over the windows—to keep out any light. He could hear the oilcloth flapping in the window to his right. He reached over until he felt it, grabbed it, gave a ferocious yank, and tore it away from the window. Light poured in. Ricardo felt his way over to the left side of the door and yanked that oilcloth off that window. More light. Now he could see the wooden floor, painted black, and a table with one chair, also painted black. And there, standing up against the black wall, dressed in simple farmer clothes, was a little old man, looking extremely scared, no more than four and a half feet tall, all wrinkly skin and bones, with white hair and an unshaven white beard. But Ricardo didn't believe that for an instant. He pulled the knife out of the scabbard that was jammed under his belt in the small of his back, pointed it toward the old man, and stepped forward. The old man eyes widened, and he screamed at the top of his lungs.

The scream startled Ricardo, and just for the briefest of a microsecond, the tiniest of synapse sparks, the thought flashed across Ricardo's mind that maybe he had been wrong—that this was the wrong house, the wrong man, an innocent old man... but then the old man lunged at Ricardo and the microsecond of doubt was gone. The little man moved fast—too fast—and knocked the knife out of Ricardo's hand and jumped on top of him, his hands at Ricardo's throat. The force of the old man's jump knocked both of them to the floor. Ricardo could feel the old man's hands wrap around his neck and squeeze. Ricardo reached out and tried to grab the old man's throat but it was suddenly too big for Ricardo to get his hands around. Ricardo looked and realized the person on top of him was not the tiny old man anymore, but was the massive brujo. And the brujo was strangling him! Ricardo could get no air in at all. He knew he only had seconds left. Ricardo reached up, grabbed both sides of the brujo's head, and jammed both thumbs into the brujo's eyes as hard as he could. The brujo screamed, released his grip on Ricardo's neck and knocked both of Ricardo's arms away from his eyes. But Ricardo used this moment to roll out from under the brujo, rolling to his right, where he saw the knife on the black floor a few feet away. Ricardo rolled over on his right side, reached out and grabbed the knife, just as the brujo jumped him from behind. Ricardo twisted to his left under the massive weight of the brujo's body and shoved the knife into the brujo's side just under the rib cage with all his might. The brujo screamed and jerked back. The force of the brujo's jerking back pulled the knife out of his side. Ricardo lost control of the knife again, and it fell to the floor.

Suddenly, the room was filled with men. They grabbed the brujo, pulled him completely off Ricardo, and they all began stabbing the brujo with long knives. The stabbings were happening just inches from Ricardo. The brujo was screaming. Panic flooded Ricardo, and he pulled himself away on the floor with both hands. Then he blinked and looked—it was don Fernando, Father Lopez, and Dan. The brujo was fighting hard but he was no match for the three men above him with knives. Each repeatedly stabbed, and kept stabbing the brujo's body even after it stopped fighting and slumped on the floor. Finally, they stopped. Dan came over and helped Ricardo up.

Father Lopez shouted out, "There is no time to waste. Take him to the pit." Don Fernando and Father Lopez each grabbed an arm and a leg of the brujo's body.

"Help us!" Father Lopez shouted to Dan and Ricardo. Dan ran over and grabbed the brujo's other arm. Without thinking, Ricardo ran over and grabbed the other leg. The four men carried the massive weight of the brujo outside. Ricardo didn't know why they were taking him outside. Were they going to call an ambulance? How did they all get there? Were they going to arrest him for stabbing the brujo? Was the brujo dead? It all was happening too fast.

"To the pit!" Father Lopez repeated, and he and don Fernando steered the group over to the edge of the brujo's yard, where the land dropped off to a garbage pit of some sort. Both don Fernando and Father Lopez simply dropped the brujo's body on the ground. Dan and Ricardo lowered their portions. Don Fernando ran around to the other side of the brujo's house. Father Lopez slid down the embankment to the garbage pit and started gathering the branches and tree limbs that were lying scattered on the ground and piling them right under the raised embankment where Ricardo and Dan stood.

Ricardo looked down at the brujo. His clothes were soaked in blood. His skin was blue-gray, his mouth open, his eyes closed. He looked dead, but there seemed to be a little movement to his chest. Ricardo realized he was still alive, gasping for air.

Don Fernando returned, running, and holding a gas can. "Hurry, hurry!" Father Lopez yelled. Don Fernando poured the gasoline from the can over the branches and other items that Father Lopez had piled below the embankment. Both don Fernando and Father Lopez stepped back from the pile and Father Lopez pulled a small box of wooden matches from his pocket, lit one and threw it on the gasoline-soaked branches and trash. Flames instantly burst up. Then both men scrambled back up the sides of the embankment to where Dan and Ricardo were standing. Ricardo took a step back. He had no idea what was going on.

Don Fernando and Father Lopez again each grabbed

an arm and a leg. Dan seemed to understand and grabbed the other arm. The three men strained to lift the brujo's body.

"Grab his leg!" Father Lopez shouted to Ricardo.

Ricardo did as he was told but finally found his voice. "What are we doing?" he shouted at Father Lopez.

"We have to fling him into the fire! Fling him into the fire before he dies!"

This made no sense to Ricardo. They were going to commit murder and burn the body. Some rational part of his brain didn't want to be a part of this, didn't want to get him into trouble, but then he realized he was being told what to do by both the only legal authority in the town and by the only moral authority in the town. Who would arrest him? Who would testify against him? No one. So, he picked up the brujo's dangling leg and together the four men lifted the brujo and swung him back to get momentum, and then flung him over the earthen ledge into the fire below. His body landed with a great cracking of tree limbs. The fire seemed to grow stronger and envelope him. Ricardo stared at his body. It seemed to twitch... yes—it moved! The flames rose around the brujo! Ricardo watched as the brujo opened his eyes, screamed loudly, and tried to get up, but he couldn't lift his wounded body. The flames were turning the brujo's flesh completely black. And then, as Ricardo watched, the brujo began to change, began to shrink, smaller and smaller, and transformed into the tiny old man that Ricardo had first seen in the house. The flames seemed to be fueled by body and burned ferociously. The intense heat finally made Ricardo turn his head away from the edge of the pit. But he looked back one more time, shielding his face from the heat, and stared down. There was a shriveled old man's body in the flames, completely black. The smell of burning flesh made him turn away again.

And as he turned away, he saw Father Lopez staring at him strangely. Father Lopez's expression was cold. He stepped up to Ricardo, stepped right up to his face, so that their bodies were almost touching, and said, "Tell me truthfully señor Ricardo, as God is your witness, did you ever have sex with him? Tell me truthfully and I promise, you will not suffer."

Ricardo was stunned and frightened by the cleric's icy tone. "No, no Padre, as God is my witness, I never had sex with him. I felt compelled to come here, and when I arrived, he attacked me."

Father Lopez's face softened. He nodded his head and glanced at the edge of the embankment where smoke was rising, and said, "We had to fling him into the fire while he was still alive. It's the only way to kill a brujo. If you had had sex with him, we would have had to do the same to you."

Ricardo felt all his muscles tighten. If he had not lied, they would have killed him!

Father Lopez walked to the edge of the pit and stared down. Don Fernando walked up and joined him.

Ricardo's mind seemed to snap, but snap in a positive way. He was no longer consumed with revenge. He felt like his old self again. He felt like he could finally think rationally. He walked back into the brujo's house, looked around, and found his knife on the floor. He picked it up, took it over to the sink, carefully washed all the blood off it, and stuck it back into the scabbard that was still under his belt in the small of his back. Then, he walked back outside.

Don Fernando and Father Lopez were still standing on the edge of the pit watching the fire. Father Lopez seemed to be saying some type of prayer and crossing himself.

Dan walked up to Ricardo and said, "Come on, we need to go. I told them I would ride with you. Come on, hurry."

They walked to Miguel's car. Dan got into the passenger side. Ricardo got into the driver's side, started the engine up, turned the car around, and started the drive back down the hill.

The two men rode in silence. Finally, Dan said, "We've been watching the house for a week, but all we saw was the old man. We never saw him as the brujo. We knew he would be calling you, so we had to wait until you came. We figured our only chance was that he would change into the brujo when you showed up."

Ricardo slammed on the brakes. He turned and shouted at Dan, "You were using me as bait?!?"

"It was the only way, man! Killing the old man would not have killed the brujo. We had to hurt him, incapacitate him when he was a brujo, and then burn him. Father Lopez said it was the only way."

"And you believed that?"

Dan just shrugged. "Sure, don't you?"

"Why didn't you tell me?!?"

"Father Lopez said we couldn't. If you knew, the brujo could have seen it in your mind when he came to you in dreams, and then we would have lost our chance. No, you had to be kept out of the loop. But we weren't going to let anything happen to you. As soon as you entered the house, we were going to rush in. And we did."

Ricardo was silent for a moment. His hands were gripping the steering wheel hard. He tried to release them. He looked out at the valley below. They were almost at the fork in the road that would lead down to the old tree. He put the car into gear and started forward, then stopped the car again and turned to Dan.

"What's going to happen now?" Ricardo asked.

"Now? Nothing. Life returns to normal. No one says anything about this, you understand? Not a word. Father Lopez and don Fernando will bury the body once it's burned. This never happened. Life will go on as normal... but this time, as really normal. No more brujo."

"Dan, do you realize we just killed someone up there?"

Dan looked at Ricardo. "Really? You don't think we were dealing with a real person up there, do you? An actual human being?"

Chapter 18:   Sleep

Ricardo slept for almost two days straight. He had dropped Dan off in Villa Rosario, then had driven to La Chorrera and returned the car to Miguel. Luckily Miguel was busy with customers and Ricardo didn't have to talk with him. He just handed the keys to the busboy and watched the busboy hand the keys to Miguel. Then he waved at Miguel and left the restaurant to catch the bus back to Villa Rosario. By the time he got back to his apartment, he was completely worn out. He had forgotten to return the knife and didn't realize that until he was already home. It was still in the sheath stuck under his belt. He washed the knife again, poured bleach on it, left it in the sink, and crawled into bed.

He slept and slept, waking only to pee, drink some water and then crawl back into bed. He had no idea why he was so exhausted. And it was not a normal kind of sleep, but rather, more like a coma, the kind of sleep that the body imposes on a person when it needs to repair some great damage. The sleep was deep, troubled at times, but deep in a way that was not sleep, but rather like floating in a different space, a different country. There were dreams, maybe, but not like regular dreams. More like shifting images and colors, all without thought, as if he was descending downward to some empty place for a while.

Finally, the second day, he opened his eyes and knew he didn't need to sleep anymore. Light was streaming into his little apartment. He got up to pee, and then splashed water on his face. He looked at the mirror. It was his face, haggard, but definitely his face. He walked into his tiny kitchen and started to make coffee. Then he realized he was weak from hunger. He opened the refrigerator and found a piece of cheese and ate that. The four or five bites of cheese seemed to jump-start his brain, and he could almost feel it starting to integrate the entire encounter with the brujo. Images began to flood his brain. He tried not to watch them and decided to take a quick shower while he waited for the coffee to brew. The hot water felt good and grounded him. He lathered up his body with soap and looked at it. The thought crossed his mind that this body of his had made love to so many people in his life, and that maybe it was possible that he might make love again. The thought pleased him and made him feel hopeful.

He got out of the shower, dried himself, shaved the edges of his beard, and then hung his towel over the metal rod of the shower and went to get dressed. He then poured himself a cup of coffee. It was then that he checked his cell phone, saw the time and the date, and realized he had slept for almost two days.

He took his coffee out onto his little patio to drink it and to think. His mind was already beginning to rationalize the brujo, to build a compartmentalized case that explained everything, a congruent explanation of events that followed in sequence, something that his brain could accept, and something that could provide a defense to all his actions. The brujo had to have been a real brujo—he had to accept that premise for any explanation to work. The brujo had been real, and when he had gone to the brujo's house, the brujo attacked him. He had stabbed the brujo only once, and that was in self-defense. It was don Fernando, the police chief, and Father Lopez, the revered old cleric of the town, and Dan, don Fernando's cohort, who had pulled the brujo off him, stabbed him repeatedly, and then forced Ricardo to help them drag the body to the fire pit and fling it over the edge into the fire. But he had seen what had happened with his own eyes—there was no denying that—the brujo had transformed back into the old man as the flames consumed him and turned him into a grotesque black twisted crisp. And what about what Father Lopez had told him about the brujo being around since before don Fernando's father was born? Maybe that meant that they hadn't killed a living person after all, in which case they hadn't committed any crime at all. Maybe Dan was right. If the brujo wasn't a living person, then they hadn't killed anyone.

Ricardo finished his first cup of coffee, went inside to refill his cup, and returned to his balcony. And besides, he reminded himself, he had the perfect defense. The police chief and the town's padre had directed him to do what he did.

But there was still the issue of the cum. He had lied to Father Lopez—and thank God he did!—about having sex with the brujo. The brujo had forced him to swallow his cum. What did that mean? He had tried to do the same thing in the bathhouse but failed, but he had succeeded the other night in his apartment. Why was the brujo so intent on that? Ricardo thought about the medical implications. Could he get a disease from that? He knew that the chances of catching HIV from swallowing semen were almost non-existent, so he wasn't worried about that. But there had to be some other reason why the brujo was so determined to make him eat his cum. Or maybe not. Maybe the brujo was just sex-obsessed. Maybe, like any other psychopathic sexual rapist/murderer, he just enjoyed raping and killing people, or enslaving them for a while as sexual slaves and then eventually killing them. It was the classic depraved psychotic pattern, throughout history. Why should the brujo be any different? Maybe he had certain psychic hypnotic powers but, like Rasputin or Ted Bundy or thousands of other psychopaths, he was just a man. Maybe that's what made him so dangerous: his singular focus for his entire adult life on finding sexual victims. But why had Father Lopez interrogated him about whether he had sex with the brujo? And what exactly did Father Lopez mean by "having sex"? Did he mean consensual, willing sex? Or did his definition include being orally raped? Maybe the priest was revealing his Catholic dogma about being tainted by desire, made impure by sex, the same as that "have to burn him while he's still alive" bullshit—part of the medieval theory of making the sinner suffer for his sins. No point in just killing him—he had to be tortured before he dies, burned at the stake, broken on the wheel, hung on a cross.

Because the fact was, Ricardo felt normal, the same as always. In fact, he felt good. His ordeal was over. He could relax. Given what had happened, and assuming everything that Jenny and Father Ricardo had told him was true—and he did believe most of it was true—the brujo was gone, and Ricardo's life would return to normal. Yes, he had been forced to swallow the brujo's cum, but it was not the first time he had been dominated, certainly not the first time he had swallowed another man's cum, and not the first time he had done so involuntarily. He was okay. He would survive this. Everything was going to be okay. His life would return to normal, to the regular routine of writing and bathhouses and brothels. He would be fine.

He got up and went inside to get a third cup of coffee. But first he stopped at this writing desk, opened up his laptop, and turned it on. Then he refilled his coffee cup while it was booting up, and then sat down at his writing desk and sent a quick email to Miguel.

"Thank you for letting me borrow your car. I really appreciate it. I still have your knife. Sorry. I forgot to return it. I will return it the next time I see you. Perhaps we can meet tomorrow at the restaurant, and I can give it to you then, and if you have time, we can walk over to our favorite steamy area."

Yes, he thought, as he hit the send button, it would be nice to visit the bathhouse again.

Chapter 19:   Normal

And Ricardo's life did return to normal. Each day started to melt into the next, like it always does in Panama. He did go see Miguel the day after he sent that email, returned the knife, thanked him profusely, and the both of them did go to the bathhouse, and they both had a very relaxing time sitting in the hot tub talking and then wandering into the darkened steam room to find people to play with. It was like old times again.

And Villa Rosario seemed to be quite normal as well. He and Dan had lunch one day and didn't even mention the burning of the brujo, except to refer to it once in passing as "that incident". Ricardo saw don Fernando a few days later in the farmer's market. Don Fernando just nodded respectfully towards him, as if they were casual acquaintances. Ricardo nodded back and continued shopping. It was as if the entire incident never occurred, exactly as Dan had predicted and recommended on the drive back from the brujo's house. Ricardo saw the logic in this, and accepted it. It felt right.

And the writing returned to normal. Over the next two weeks he finished a few more short stories and sent them off to his publisher. His publisher called him a few days after that and said he had enough to release another book of short stories. And that pleased Ricardo.

And one afternoon a few days after that, Ricardo was thinking about writing another novel, and he was daydreaming about topics, when he opened up the "Maybe" file on his desktop and starting reading through pages and ideas and drafts of various subjects that he had started but for one reason or another had put aside. And he came across the pages he had written on *The Old Man and the Semen* and he read them and remembered he had liked them. He knew his publisher hated the title, but they could discuss that later. Maybe he could develop that idea. So he printed out his pages and placed them on his desk to re-read in the morning.

And that evening he, for some reason, started to think about Carolina. He wondered whatever had happened to her and Leslie, and what had happened to the big investigation at the University. So he made a note to email her the next morning also.

And he sat out on his patio that night, and drank a glass or two of Sangría, and he thought, what a strange and mysterious world this is, that despite all his years of keeping his sexual identity undercover, despite the years of hiding his writing life from his business colleagues, and despite the years of drinking and rehab stints, and feeling so often at the end of his rope, he had somehow made it to this little town in this little country where he could write and where he could pursue his physical desires quietly and happily. He was lucky to still be alive, and he knew that. He quietly raised his glass to the dark sky as a toast and took a sip.

And he thought again about Carolina and wondered again how she was doing. He thought about how beautiful she was, and how he had always wanted to explore that body of hers, but it had just never worked out. The age difference was just too much for her, and he had always understood that and had not pressed the issue. But he also knew that people change, and that the older she got, the age difference might not seem so insurmountable. He thought about this for a few minutes, and then amused himself by mentally visualizing himself slowlyunbuttoning her blouse, one button at a time, to expose what he assumed—because he had never seen her naked—were plump round breasts with tiny pink nipples. Pity that Leslie was having first crack at them, caressing them, touching them, running her fingers up to those points, then bending down to gently kiss, nuzzle, and suck those nipples while her fingers explored areas further south. He thought about this for a while and wondered what sounds Carolina might make during sex. Would she moan softly? Or make louder gasping noises? He would certainly like to find out, he thought to himself.

He finished his glass of Sangría, and went inside, locked the door, rinsed out his glass and got ready to go to bed. Once in bed he closed his eyes and quickly fell asleep. And he began to dream.

*　　*　　*

And in his dream he and Carolina were at a noisy nightclub. They were sitting close at a small table in the corner away from the crowd, but even there it was loud. Music from the stage was blaring over the speakers, and people were dancing in front of the stage. Both he and Carolina were drinking martinis out of martini glasses and laughing and trying to shout at each other to be heard. Ricardo realized that they were sitting so close to each other that he had his arm around her, and her hand was on his thigh to support herself. She was smiling and looking at him and having a good time. He leaned forward and kissed her. Her small mouth was wet and open, and she kissed him back. Then she pulled her head back and smiled at him again. Then she leaned back in, putting both hands on his thighs for support, and they kissed again, this time longer. He dabbed his tongue gently into her mouth and she did the same to him. He reached both his arms around her shoulders and held her close. She released hands from his thighs and reached around his waist and squeezed him.

After a few more kisses, he shouted over the din, "I wish there was somewhere we could go."

She yelled back, "I know a place," and grabbed his hand and stood up.

She led the way, away from the dance floor, through a hallway, down a corridor, where they stepped into a dark room. It was amazingly quiet, except for the hissing of the steam radiators along the wall. There was a single window and an old couch. The moonlight coming through the

163

window gave the room a warm soft yellow glow.

"What is this room?" Ricardo asked.

"It's just a room they never use," she said and stepped in close to him.

They kissed again. He ran his hands up and down her body, while she wrapped her arms around him. He realized she was wearing jeans. He ran his right hand down the outside of her thigh and then up her inner thigh, slowing down as he passed over her crotch, and then pressing into her crotch, moving back between her legs.

"Let's sit down," she said, and they went over to the old couch and fell onto it. Somehow her blouse had gotten untucked from her jeans and he ran his hand up under it and over her stomach and up to her bra as they kissed and held each other. She ran her hand over his crotch. He was getting hard. She reached down and unbuckled his belt...

*   *   *

He awoke the next morning with a vivid recollection of the dream. He must have just dreamed it right before he had woken up, he thought—it was so vivid. He lay there reliving it, the soft hot feel of her flesh, the enthusiasm with which she wanted him. What a weird place, some kind of old-style discotheque.

He got up and made coffee. Some mornings he liked to just lie in bed and drink one or two cups of coffee before getting up, but other mornings, like today, he was energized and wanted to get started on the day. So, he took a shower while his coffee was brewing, and after drying and getting dressed, took his coffee cup out to his little patio.

He had much to do today. His publisher had sent him a list of possible cover shots for the new book. He wanted to re-read the *Old Man* pages that he had printed out yesterday and see if he could do something with them. He wanted to email a hello to Carolina. And if he got a lot of work done today, he might even reward himself with a trip to Jenny's that evening.

After a small breakfast of fruit and cereal, Ricardo

worked for several hours. First, he spent time rereading the *Old Man* pages, and then started typing out some new descriptions, and new plot angles... He liked what he was writing; it had possibilities. Later that morning he selected two photos he liked from the ones his publisher had sent him for the book cover of short stories, and he sent his comments about them to his publisher along with a note describing his new ideas for developing the *Old Man* story. He even reluctantly asked his publisher to suggest another name. After he sent that email, he decided to take a break, maybe walk downtown for some lunch. He had just taken his empty coffee cup to the sink when the ding of his incoming email called him back to his desk. He looked at the screen and then sat down. It was an email from Carolina.

His heart began to pound a bit. How weird was this? He opened her email and read:

Hey there. Sorry I've been so out of touch. It's all been so crazy that I haven't had any time to write. Leslie and I finally broke up, and she moved out. I was broken-hearted for a while until I discovered that she had been feeding information to the dean who was leading the investigation. But then the dean's wife discovered his emails back and forth to Leslie, and the wife raised such a stink that the school has dropped the investigation. Turned out the dean had a thing for Leslie. What a fucked-up situation!

Anyway, I started missing you terribly last night, and I realized I felt so bad getting so distracted from our friendship. I don't know what I was doing with Leslie. That was insane. Listen, I know I said I wanted to come down and visit, and then I said I didn't, but now I really do again. I hope you're not mad at me. Is there any possibility I could come down and stay with you during spring break after all? It's only two weeks away, I know, and this is short notice, but I can still buy tickets. I don't care what they cost. I just realize I miss you and want to see you.

Love,

Carolina

Ricardo sat back stunned. Was this possible? He forced himself to take a deep breath. He re-read the email, thought for another minute, and then typed a reply:

Would love to see you. Come on down.
Love,
Ricardo

Carolina had never signed off her emails with "Love" before, but since she had done it this time, he figured he might as well return the favor. He thought about reminding her of what he had said weeks earlier about sharing a bed but decided not to say anything. He had already told her once. It would be her problem to deal with now. He hit the send button.

Wow, he thought. What a coincidence! He got up and retrieved his empty coffee cup from the sink, refilled it with cold coffee from the coffee pot, microwaved it, and took it out to his balcony.

He sat and sipped at his coffee and thought about what had just happened. Sometimes, he thought, when two people are in synchronicity, they can start thinking about each other at the same time. That's not unusual. His whole dream last night and her saying that she was thinking about him last night—that kind of thing happens all the time. People think it's fate, or some sort of long distance telepathy, but who knows? Anyway, weird as it was, he was glad. As he sat there, a certain darker thought began to nag at him, but then he heard the ding of his computer email again. He went back inside.

This time the email was from Marta.

Hey you. Just checking in. Hadn't heard from you in a while. Tom and I just got back from a hiking trip in Colorado. How are you? How's the writing? Any plans to come to the States, maybe next Christmas? Would love to see you.

Besos,
Marta

This email made him smile. He loved Marta so much. And additionally, this email dispelled his earlier darker thought. You see, he said to himself, I didn't dream about Marta last night and she was thinking of me, too. Friends who are on the same wavelength, the same life rhythms simply think about each other at similar times. His dream about Carolina and the timing of her email were just coincidental. He started a reply message to Marta.

I'm doing great. Just finished a new book of short stories. Should be out in a few months. I've just restarted working on that Old Man and the Semen book again. I had put it aside for a while, but suddenly I'm re-enthused about it. No specific plans for Christmas, but I might be able to fit a trip in sometime this year, maybe when the rains come here. It would be good to see you again, as always."
Besos baby,
Ricardo

He thought about what a lighthouse Marta had always been for him. It was good to have friends like her. He hit the send button.

A second later, the incoming email bell dinged again. What is this, he thought, Grand Central Station? He never got this much email in one morning. He looked. It was another email from Carolina. She had booked her flights, and the email contained her arrival and departure times. She added a line about being excited to see him, and signed off with "Love" once again. He replied back, saying he would make arrangements to meet her at the airport and was likewise looking forward to seeing her.

Ricardo took down his wall calendar from the wall and marked the dates of Carolina's flights on it. He would have to arrange transportation from Panama City airport to Villa Rosario. Normally he just took a series of buses when he flew in, but for Carolina maybe he would splurge and have Minor take him to the airport to pick her up and bring them back.

He looked at the dates when she would be there. He had two weeks until then. Maybe, he thought... maybe tonight he would try and dream about Marco. Two weeks would be more than enough time to pull Marco away from whatever he was doing for a bit, maybe take him down to Hotel de Sevilla for a few days, or maybe just bring him to the apartment for a night or two.

Why not? One last fling indeed. Maybe a couple of last flings.

-FIN-

ABOUT THE AUTHOR

Robert Rahula was born in Spain to an American father and Spanish mother, but grew up in Virginia on the farm of his paternal grandparents. He returned to Menorca, Spain, in the 1960s to pursue his writing career. These days he travels in Europe, Central and South America for several months a year, giving readings and lectures, and spends the rest of his time writing, dividing his time between Spain and the United States.

Over the past thirty years, Robert has published dozens books of prose and poetry in Spain and in the United States. While he remains relatively undiscovered in the United States, he is revered in Spain as the founder of the "portilla" style of popular Spanish poetry: non-metered fluid verse that deals with love, loss, bisexuality, separateness, and growing older.

All of Robert's novels are available in English, including his groundbreaking erotic novel *Messieurs*; his second English novel *Panamaniac*; his erotic murder mystery *Island of Misfits*; his "sexistential" novel *Conversations in a Belgian Bar*; his magical realism novella *Day Another Paradise In*; his memoir novel *A Modest Summation of Things*; as well as his "Dan Landes Mystery" novels: *Bathhouse Stories, All the Yage in Reno, Exigent Circumstances*, and *Uninvited Guest*.

Eight volumes of Robert's English poetry are also available: *Trigger Points; Inside the Locked Heart; Camino; Migration; I Sing the Body Politic; Wonderland; From Whose Bourn; Expat Poems*; an anthology of his English poems and short stories, *Half-Life*; and a collection of his most famous Spanish poems, *Poemas Españoles*. Other poems, along with his blog on writing and his tour itinerary, appear on his Facebook page and on his website robertrahula.com.